Death of a Dummy

(A Wax Museum Mystery)

by

C. F. Carter

For information, email **Cozy Cat Press**, cozycatpress@aol.com or visit our website at: www.cozycatpress.com

COZY CAT
P R E S S

ISBN: 978-1-939816-77-1

Printed in the United States of America

Cover by Paula Ellenberger
http://www.paulaellenberger.com/design

1 2 3 4 5 6 7 8 9 10

For Kerry, Ariel, and the people of Old Québec.
Thank you for the support and inspiration.

Prologue

The hand holding the cigarette was deeply tanned and rough like old leather.

I watched, transfixed, while an impossibly long ribbon of smoke stretched to the ceiling. Nothing in the silent and suffocating room moved enough to disturb the air. Even the clinking from the bottling plant beyond the door, and the rumblings of the winery's harvesting machines were muted by triple-glazed windows.

I was visiting my father, Elroy Wainscott, in his office on our country estate in Vancouver. I spent my winters there, working just enough hours in the family winery to finance my next surf adventure. But in the summer when the waves started pumping, I would cast off the trappings of wealth and rent a place with easy access to the beach—a place where I could go feral for awhile, and forget about wine and business.

I cleared my throat nervously. "You ready?"

My dad raised his cigarette and inhaled, squinting through the smoke with one eye while studying me through the other. His gaze began at my sandals, moved past my tanned legs and board shorts, and stopped at my unbuttoned shirt where mirrored sunglasses hung instead of a necktie. His free hand rested on a bulging white envelope. "Relax. We're waiting for your brother-in-law."

"We don't need to wait—" I started, but broke off as the door cracked open to reveal a beaming face with pearly white teeth and a hairnet.

It was Todd, the living Ken Doll himself. *Winery Ken.*

My dad waved him in with a huge smile. "Come in, my boy! Paul's going to pitch us one of his business ideas."

Winery Ken was decked out for a day at the Barbie bottling plant with a smartly pressed lab coat, a Brooks Brothers suit, and a pocket *pH* meter tucked in his breast pocket that he didn't have the foggiest idea how to use. He carefully removed his hairnet and combed his golden hair back into a smooth shell. Then he dragged a chair around the ponderous mahogany desk to sidle up next to my dad.

It's true what they say about nature abhorring a vacuum. Two short weeks after I'd left for my beach house, Todd had gotten a job at the winery and moved into my old room. A few weeks later, he'd convinced my sister to marry him. And now, he was being groomed for the managerial role in the family business that was meant for me.

He was dropping in on my wave, and that's not cool.

My dad watched him like an infatuated schoolgirl, then returned his attention to me. "I've asked for Todd's input. He has a good head for business."

I remembered pulling the heads off my sister's Ken dolls. "Todd didn't even finish high school. He cleans our effluent filters."

"Used to clean them," my dad corrected. "Todd applied himself. While you were out playing, he learned my business and climbed his way to the top."

"He's been here a month!"

Todd examined his fingernails absently, but I could tell he was enjoying this. My dad had invited him just to get under my skin. He'd never agreed with my high-risk, high-reward mindset, and maintained that the only sure way to double your money was to fold it in half and stick it in your pocket. But I preferred to work smarter, not harder, and it drove him nuts.

Dad looked at me wearily and stubbed out his cigarette. "Now, what do you want my money for this time?" He leaned back and folded his arms, exchanging a furtive smirk with Todd.

It was worse than I'd expected. Somehow I'd become the butt of their private joke. I imagined them puffing on fat cigars at the country club, sharing a brandy and a hearty laugh at my expense. I'd forgotten to bring the stress toy that my psychologist told me to squeeze when I felt angry. So I squeezed the laser pointer in my pocket instead and heard a sharp crack.

I gathered up my transparencies and stood to begin my presentation, but my dad stopped me with a raised hand. "Just summarize it. We're on a tight schedule, and there's something we need to discuss afterwards."

"Okay," I began, feeling my throat tighten. "As you know, the bio-fuel industry is totally pumping right now. My idea is to harvest methane gas from cows using special collection tanks and a tube inserted into... well, you know."

Todd furrowed his eyebrows and tilted his head, "I'd like to hear this, Paul. Where does the tube go?"

My dad rubbed his face. "Never mind, I've heard enough."

I finally broke that calm veneer of his—the one that always began with him listening politely to my dubious business proposal, and ended with a Big Fat Check to shut me up. He wasn't a sucker. He was tough, and could rip apart any business plan. But he felt extra responsible for my success since he'd forced me to get my business diploma after art school.

But this time, his checkbook was nowhere in sight. He flicked the envelope across his polished desk.

I turned it over. "What's this?"

"It's not a cow fart. That's for damn sure."

He was right. It was an old brass key and a mortgage agreement made out in my name. "You bought me a house in Quebec?"

"It's an investment property. A *real* business, not one of your get-rich-quick schemes. If you get some solid tenants and don't bungle things up, it'll provide you with a steady income. There's a pre-paid credit card in there with enough money to cover your expenses and mortgage for three months. But when the money runs out, that's it."

"He's serious," Todd chimed in. "Not another cent."

Another cracking sound came from my pocket.

My dad continued, "Just so we're clear—if you don't turn a profit in three months, Todd will fly down and clean up your mess, and you'll return home to work at the winery."

I arched an eyebrow. "And if I succeed?"

"Then you're free to do what you like. Keep the building, sell it to finance another business, I don't care. But I'd like to see you stick with it for awhile. Who knows? You might even be happy there."

I stared at the envelope and didn't move.

Todd checked his watch, then headed for the door. "We better get to the country club, Dad. Our tee-off is in ten minutes."

Did he just say Dad?

I snatched up the envelope and put on my shades.

That had just made my decision a whole lot easier.

Chapter 1

After spending a week in a cramped van with a damp Golden Retriever, I had hoped to be greeted with a sunrise. But when I finally passed through the stone gates of Quebec City, it was just another overcast and drizzling morning.

Events of the past weeks played back in my mind. My dad was clearly surprised when I'd accepted his fool's errand. There was no way he thought that his slacker son would give up his primo beach house and a summer of spicy mamas—for a place that was four hundred miles from the nearest surfable wave. Maybe if his head wasn't always stuck in a wine barrel, he'd know me better.

I parked my van and let Beachley out, pausing to check my reflection in a store window. Against a backdrop of elegant storefronts and curious pedestrians in business attire, I was clearly out of my natural habitat. With long, sun-bleached hair and my skin covered in misguided tattoos, I looked like one of those knuckleheads they chase out of food joints near the beach.

And if I was being honest, I *was* one of those knuckleheads.

I tied Beachley up under the awning of a cozy looking restaurant and headed inside to grab a bite and look through my emails.

French folk music, the clatter of dishes and conversation filled the small room, along with an overpowering, smoky aroma of pancakes and bacon.

The warm ambiance was enhanced considerably by the dark and drizzly sky outside. Exhausted, I sank onto an open stool at the counter, where camera-toting tourists watched authentic French-Canadian ladies prepare their food right in front of them.

I studied the cook nearest to me while she took care of another customer. She skillfully deposited a crêpe onto the customer's plate, scrunching her freckled nose as if to fight an itch. Like the other girls at the crêpe counter, she wore a *Crème de la Crêpe* tee shirt, with a bandana wrapped around her head to act as a hairnet. She turned to me and smiled sweetly. "Bonjour."

"Morning!" I replied in French.

I was suddenly grateful for the French immersion school system. I had fiercely resisted it, but relented when my folks had said it was either that or home-schooling. Even so, that was a few years back, so my pronunciation was sketchy at best.

She stood patiently, shifting her weight from foot to foot. When I realized she was waiting for my order, I gave her my dimpliest smile. "What do you recommend?"

"Hmm. A crêpe?"

"Sweet! I'll have one of those."

"What kind?" she asked, gesturing at the chalkboard behind her.

The large board had dozens of crêpe varieties written on it. They all looked super tasty, and my stomach was growling. There were a dozen solid breakfast options to consider, but I felt rushed by her body language. She crossed her arms and tilted her head to one side, locking her blue eyes on me.

I read her nametag. "Just make me your personal favorite. Give me the *Sophie Special*."

I watched as she poured a large scoop of batter onto the crêpe pan, then swirled it into a thin, perfect crêpe using a rake-like spatula. "Check you out!" I said, shaking my head. "You've got skills!"

She smiled faintly.

A large family in matching yellow ponchos passed behind my stool, kicking and trampling over my bags repeatedly without a glance back. I could hardly blame them; in the packed restaurant there really wasn't room for my duffel bags.

I picked up my smaller bag and held it over the counter. Red liquid dripped from the seams.

Sophie noticed, and her spatula stopped moving. "It looks like blood. Do I want to know what you keep in there?"

Every customer within earshot looked at me, and then at my bag. I was surprised at how many people overheard our conversation. Then again, it was such a small room it was almost impossible not to. And I had to admit the word *blood* was a superb attention grabber.

"It's not blood," I sighed. "Except maybe in a biblical sense. It's wine."

Satisfied that I wasn't a serial killer, the other patrons turned back to their breakfast and their own conversations.

I grabbed a handful of napkins and wiped up the small dark puddle forming in front of me. I unzipped the bag and found the broken remains of a bottle that once had contained dark, full-bodied red claret. My mom had stuffed it in there as a reminder of our family winery. And now it was destined for a trashcan. Quite poetic, if I thought about it.

Sophie flipped the crêpe over. It was a thing of beauty. Golden brown and as thin as a sheet of parchment paper. Without looking up, she asked, "So, are you staying in the building across the street? I saw you arrive out front."

I felt pleased that she'd noticed me, even if it was only because of my out-of-place beach attire. She probably saw hundreds of better looking dudes every day: fancy Frenchmen with wind-tousled hair, high cheekbones and silk scarves. I was a transplanted surf junkie—a fish out of water in every sense.

"Actually, I'm the new owner. It's an investment property."

Her face brightened. "Nice! So where are you from?"

"Vancouver. But just so you know, I'm not one of those hippies who go on long hikes and eats bark."

"And I'm not a crazy driver who eats cheese and chain smokes," Sophie replied with a laugh. "I'd love to visit Vancouver some day to take pictures."

"You're a photographer?"

"Well, sorta. It's just a hobby. I'm into artsy black and white stuff, so most of my images come off moody and depressing. But the ones you see on the wall here are my lighter ones. I call them my happy accidents." She pointed to a series of black and white photos nearby.

I studied them approvingly. "Meeting you today was a happy accident."

She smiled and rolled her eyes. Then she grabbed handfuls of roast beef, ham, cheese, and green peppers and sprinkled them on the crêpe. "I can tell you like cheese, so I gave you extra."

I laughed. "I guess that was pretty lame, wasn't it? You're good for my mood, though. I've been driving in a hot van for days with a blown motor, and it rained the whole way. So it's nice to see a friendly face."

"You must have brought the rain with you, it's been clear and sunny for weeks." She flipped and folded the crêpe and slid it onto my plate, adding a small paper cup of maple syrup. There you go, I hope you like it.

Sophie on a plate."

"Sophie looks great," I said, making eye contact and smiling.

She looked embarrassed, so I turned my attention to my crêpe. I cut off a large piece, drizzled it with maple syrup and popped it in my mouth. I shook my head in disbelief as I chewed. "Man, this is one tasty pancake!"

"I'm glad you like it." She turned her head to the entrance, and her smile faded.

"What's wrong?" I asked.

She nodded toward an unshaven, scowling man who'd just entered the restaurant. "That's the caretaker of your building. His name is Napoleon Roy."

I've read that in the evolutionary chain, all life is linked, from the lowliest slugs, to hairy beasts, and finally to modern man. The missing link who stood in the doorway fell somewhere in the middle. Hairy forearms poked through a black garbage bag with holes cut in the sides—and beneath, a wild nest of grey hair, and two red-rimmed eyes darted around the room in search of a free seat, or maybe his next murder victim.

I shrugged. "Napoleon, eh? It suits him."

She leaned forward and lowered her voice. "Watch out for him. If you ask me..." She twirled her finger around her ear.

"He has vertigo?"

"No, I'm saying he's a bit crazy."

"Don't worry," I said. "I'll jettison that kook in due time. A guy like him has no place in the hospitality industry. I can't afford to pay him, anyway."

"Well if you need anything, you can ask the former owner, Guy Tremblay. He has the antique shop next door. He's really nice; he comes in for coffee every morning before opening, so he's probably there now if you want to say hello."

"Great, I'll probably do that," I said. "You rock,

Sophie."

She smiled and turned to take another customer's order.

I rushed through the remainder of my meal and left my payment on the counter, including a generous tip. Then on impulse, I bought an assortment of chocolates and pastries to go.

I'd just keep track of the calories in my head and jog them off later.

I rejoined Beachley and took a fresh look at my new digs.

It was still early and most of the street was in shadows, but the sun peeked through the clouds and lit up my building like Saint Elmo's Fire. It was a well maintained two-story stone building, with overflowing flower baskets and stone gables. Copper flashing around the shuttered windows glinted in the morning light. Over time, the copper would have the same green patina as the roof—but I was pretty sure I wouldn't be around when it happened.

Still, I was impressed, and couldn't believe it was all mine.

I felt more than a little guilty. My parents must have spent a fortune on this historic building. Given my track record, they must have known I'd be laying down rubber when the ninety-day trial was up—my own Sword of Damocles. Either they hoped it would be long enough to make me forget about my friends and my old life, or long enough to make me forge stronger ties on this end of the country. Either way, they were desperate for me to succeed, and clearly had an inflated opinion of this city.

I jogged across the wet cobblestones, leaving Beachley under the awning while I unlocked the door.

Newspapers were taped to the inside of the storefront window. Beside it, a freshly painted door probably led to apartments upstairs. Next to an old buzzer, the label *Caretaker* was scratched out and *Owner* written in its place. With an unexpected glimmer of pride, I realized that both of these monikers belonged to me.

I took a breath and slid my key in the lock, but it wouldn't turn.

The number on the building clearly matched the one printed on the key tag, and there were no other keyholes in sight. Thanks to Sophie, I knew where I could get a spare.

I dashed through the rain and ducked into Tremblay Antiques.

I was taken aback by the smell of lemon wax and pipe smoke. When my eyes adjusted to the dim light, I was stunned.

I had expected a typical antique store with ratty old furniture, worn carpets, and shelves full of yard sale bric-a-brac. Tremblay's had none of these things. In fact, I'd never seen such a display of wealth.

Golden belt plates and full suits of armor hung from the ceiling. Unusual artifacts made from every type of precious metal filled the shelves and formed towering displays. Bronze weapons, ancient chests and exotic furnishings were everywhere, and all of it sparkled under halogen lighting.

Surrounded by such a treasure hoard one would almost expect to see a fire-breathing dragon, or even King Midas himself. Instead, I saw a plump old man reading a newspaper, scratching his stomach through a T-shirt that read *Vintage, Not Old*.

"Are you the owner?" I asked.

He glanced up from his paper and a look of surprise crossed his face. He stood with the help of a cane and smiled, holding out his hand. "Well, if it isn't little Paul Wainscott! You're all grown up now!"

I instinctively glanced around to see if another Paul Wainscott was standing nearby, then shook his hand while scrutinizing his face. "Have we met before?"

He chuckled and shook his head. "I can't blame you for forgetting me. Last time you saw me, I was younger and thinner. I'm Guy Tremblay, an old friend of your parents." He took a step back for a better look, then winked at me. "If it makes you feel any better, I wouldn't have recognized you either. But your father sent me a lot of pictures over the years. He says a lot of great things about you."

Now I was *convinced* he had the wrong person. My dad could write a list of my good points on a sticky note with a wide-tip marker and still have room left over.

I searched my memory. I'd only been to Quebec once when I was very young; my family had rented a place right here in the old city. I'd seen Polaroids in my mother's photo album, but I was too little then to remember any details. My tired mind was swirling, and I felt a bit annoyed that my dad was discussing my private life with strangers.

I forced a smile. "They never mentioned you. How did you become pen pals?"

Guy walked to the sales counter, beckoning with his finger for me to follow. He produced a handful of faded photographs from a drawer and spread them over the counter. "Years before opening Tremblay Antiques, I spent every penny I had on the building you just bought. I converted the main floor into a gift shop, and rented rooms to vacationers. You and your parents stayed there for almost two months. Since I was acting as the hotelier, maid, handyman, and shop clerk, I saw your parents every day. They were very kind, and we became fast friends. I even had you all out to my cottage."

Guy tapped one of the photos. "Do you remember driving to my cottage in this van?"

I immediately recognized the Volkswagen Westphalia in the picture. "No way! That looks exactly like my van."

Guy's eyes twinkled. "So it is. I sold it to your parents. Your dad loved the freedom it represented and wanted to drive it home himself. You took the train home with your mother."

I was speechless, and not just because he'd described my dad as a free spirit. My banged-up van was one of the most important things in my life. My father gave it to me on the day I earned my driver's license. I wondered how much my hippie van had contributed to my love of surfing, and whether my dad regretted giving it to me now. In a way, I felt we shared the blame for my apathetic lifestyle; my dad, for giving me everything I'd asked for, and me, because I kept on asking. I focused on surfing every day simply because I could.

Guy showed me a picture of a skinny little dude in a tidal pool with his jeans rolled up. "You would spend hours searching for tadpoles while I enjoyed long chats with your parents. They wanted to learn French, so I refused to speak any English to them. They said they would retire here one day and open a bed and breakfast." Guy shook his head, lost in his memories. "How you cried when you had to leave!"

I couldn't imagine my parents being so whimsical. The photos brought up more questions than they answered. Why didn't my father tell me he knew the previous owner of the building? Was there more to my being here than an income opportunity? He could have set me up with a business anywhere in the country, even in Vancouver, where he could have kept a closer eye on me. Was there something about this building, this lifestyle, that he was hoping I would embrace because he wasn't able to?

Guy seemed to read my mind. "I was thrilled to hear from your father when he called about finding you an investment property. I'd thought about selling, but even though I've had generous offers, I wanted to be sure the new owner would appreciate its beauty and history. And from what your father tells me, I expect you will."

He snorted with laughter and slapped his knee. "And if it bothers that traitorous ex-wife of mine, so much the better! She's been trying to get her hooks into that building for years."

I wondered what his reaction would be if he knew I was only there on a trial basis, that the building would be resold if I failed to turn a profit in the next three months. Now I had two incentives to succeed: my father's respect, and protecting Guy's legacy, who I was really starting to like. Actually, three, if I counted living three thousand miles away from the annoying Todd.

"Well," I said, looking around the store, "it looks like you have your hands full. You've done really well for yourself. This place is incredible."

"It's an obsession, Paul. It really is. If I come across a rare item, I need to acquire it at any cost. It's more important to me than money. But as they say, when you follow your passions, the money invariably follows."

I knew that Guy was right, although it probably helped if your passion related to business. Even surfers could get rich by snagging a big sponsor. But I was grounded enough to realize that for most, it was a pipe dream—literally and figuratively. Unrewarded talent is almost a proverb, and I refused to be a cliché.

I said, "It must be harder now with the internet, with hundreds of people bidding on every item."

"You're right. Once an item goes online it's almost impossible to get it for a price that leaves room for resale. So I've had to adjust my tactics over the years."

"You mean burglary?" I teased, grinning widely.

He shooed the idea away with his hand. "Oh, nothing like that. But in business, one needs to blur ethical lines sometimes." He sighed deeply and smiled. "Anyway, I love everything here. If I could lock the door and never sell another item, I'd die a happy man."

"You could convert this to a museum and charge admission," I joked.

"That's not a half-bad idea, my boy. I have treasures that a museum would kill for. Stop by tomorrow and I'll give you the grand tour." He lowered his voice and winked. "I'll even show you my private collection."

"Great! I'll be here."

I noticed some great-looking doorknockers next to the sales counter. One was an antique brass design shaped like a woman's head with long flowing hair. I handed it to Guy. I'll buy this if you can part with it. It looks kind of like me."

Guy laughed and said, "Good choice. I like knockers, too. You can have it, my friend. But I do need to update my inventory." He turned to his computer and started typing.

I peered over his shoulder. "You have all these items in the store typed into a spreadsheet or something?"

"Actually, this is my new point-of-sale system. It handles sales, inventory, reports, and even does my taxes. It took over a year and a dozen part-time students to enter all the items."

As Guy put the knocker into a bag and handed it to me, I remembered why I'd come. "Do you have a spare key to my building? Mine doesn't fit the lock."

Guy narrowed his eyes and turned to the back of the store. "Napoleon!"

A hulking man in denim overalls moseyed over from the next aisle, where apparently he'd been eavesdropping.

It was the Cro-Magnon from the crêperie—the same fat nose, same square jaw, and the same look of bottled-up rage. Napoleon sneered at me while he argued with Guy in a low voice. Finally, he tossed a set of keys on the counter and addressed me in clipped English, "You owe me for the new locks."

"Who asked you to change the locks?" Guy asked him.

"With a new owner," Napoleon said, drizzling contempt on the word *owner*, "one should always change the locks."

He smirked and headed for the back of the store.

"I apologize for Napoleon," Guy said quietly. "But what can I do? He has a special talent for acquiring antiques. He is one of the *pure laine*, or pure wool. His family tree goes back to our founding fathers, and he takes that very seriously. To him, you're a second-class citizen if your mother tongue is English—it doesn't matter how well you speak French. And, of course, he's now without a place to live. He was staying in your building in exchange for doing maintenance work."

I was confused. "So all that anger is over language differences?"

"Well, not entirely," Guy said, shaking his head. "He's been having family problems, too."

Now that was something I could relate to. "Maybe I could have a talk with him and smooth things over?"

"You could certainly try. Napoleon plays Pétanque in the park with his friends every afternoon. Now that it's summer, they usually strip down and wear Speedos. Believe me, you can't miss them."

"That can't be good for tourism."

We enjoyed a good laugh, and something shattered

in the back of the store.

Napoleon Roy's ears must have been as big as his nose.

I pocketed the keys and headed for the door, ready to check out my new building. "Thanks, Guy. See you tomorrow."

Guy smiled and patted me on the back. "Remember, I'm here if you need anything. I'm really glad to get to know you again, Paul. You and I will take care of each other, no?"

"You bet. I'll be back soon."

Chapter 2

Even though the rain was warm, a cold breeze from the Laurentian mountains made Beachley tremble against my leg while she waited for me to open the door.

This time, it unlocked with a welcoming click.

It took a moment for my eyes to adjust to the dark interior. I pulled down the newspapers covering the windows, bathing the dusty room in light for what might have been the first time in years. Exposed stone walls with empty shelves stretched up to a decorative carved ceiling. The only furniture in the room was a sales counter and a display case.

Behind a bead curtain, I discovered a drawing room, with an enormous fireplace and leather chairs on one end and a small kitchenette on the other. The walls were covered in dark wooden panels, the type one finds in stately manor houses and castles.

An antique leather reservation book was open on a side table. I was no expert on the hospitality industry— at least not yet—but I was pretty sure there was an online service I could use to make managing reservations a whole lot easier than using a hand-bound relic. Some of them might even include a customizable turn-key website. I needed to get organized as quickly as possible.

I was encouraged to see that most of the rooms in the book were blocked out for the rest of the summer, and that there were even reservations around Christmas. Assuming that the rooms were priced properly, I had a good feeling that making a profit would be a walk in the park.

I returned to the front room and noticed a flight of stairs leading to the apartments.

"I'm going to check upstairs," I told Beachley. "Stay here and call me if anyone touches our stuff."

She promptly rested her front paws on the bags. If anyone touched my things, Beachley would bark. I'd taught her that trick so she could guard my stuff on the beach while I was surfing.

The rental units upstairs were either studios or single-bed apartments with a kitchen and bathroom. Napoleon must have been squatting in the larger one facing the street, since it had a musty smell and litter on the floor that indicated someone had left in a hurry.

Given what I'd seen in the reservation book, I was surprised to see that most of the units were vacant. My earlier optimism faded. I wondered if it was typical to have so many cancellations this close to a major tourist festival. If so, I was in serious trouble.

My first order of business was to clean and fix up the apartments, and add a few amenities to make them more attractive to renters. After that, I'd call some of the past tenants and get their feedback. Before I'd left Vancouver, I'd made a quick Internet search, and discovered that my property wasn't listed anywhere. These days, if you have no online presence, you may as well not exist.

I jumped when a door opened next to me.

A young man stepped into the hallway dressed like a bronze sculpture. Bronze makeup covered his hands and face, matching the color of his clothes. Even his eyes looked bronze—a disconcerting effect I assumed was due to contact lenses. If he stood perfectly still, I doubted I could tell him apart from a real statue.

"Hello," the man said in a soft voice. "You must be

the new owner. I'm Remy St. Claire."

I offered my hand. "Nice to meet you. I'm Paul Wainscott."

Remy showed me his hands with a sheepish grin. "I probably shouldn't shake; I might get makeup on you."

I caught a glimpse of bare skin and tattoos under Remy's sleeves. I also caught a whiff of marijuana in the air around him. The newly-minted businessperson in me felt that Remy might not be the ideal tenant, but at the same time, my surfer side refused to be judgmental.

That fact was, Remy reminded me of my friends back home.

"I guess you're heading to work now?" I asked.

Remy looked uneasy. "Yes, and I'll have your rent this week for sure. You probably know that I'm a few months behind."

I waved a hand in the air. "We'll discuss that later; I haven't even been through the books yet. I was just going to say that it's raining and you might need an umbrella, especially wearing all that makeup."

I made a mental note to check on his back rent. The clock was ticking and I needed revenue, not another friend.

Remy grinned and visibly relaxed. "It's waterproof, but thanks."

I gestured around me. "Where are all the other renters? It can't be just you?"

"I'm afraid so. It was very busy a few weeks ago. After everyone left, nobody new arrived to replace them. It just sort of emptied out."

Things were getting worse by the minute. I went from having a fully-occupied building, to just one tenant who didn't pay his rent. A seed of doubt in my mind grew, but I forced it out before it could take root. Todd's smug face flashed in my mind. Failure was not an option.

"In that case," I said, "I'll need some rent soon after all. Just pay what you can and we'll chip away at the balance."

"Thank you," Remy said, smiling. "I've been working a lot of hours so I'll be able to pay something tomorrow for sure." He paused. "I hope you don't take this the wrong way, but you look young. Did you major in business?"

"I prefer to think of myself as a fine arts graduate," I replied. "I earned a business diploma afterwards. There aren't many opportunities for a guy with an arts degree who looks like I do."

Remy said, "I have a degree in performance arts, and look what I do for a living. But now that I have this new gig, I'll be making twice as much money."

It occurred to me that the only thing separating us were my wealthy parents. If not for them, I might be doing caricatures on the street for spare change too.

"What's your other act?" I asked.

"I'm a mime."

"Like Marcel Marceau?"

"Exactly! He's one of my heroes. I always work in front of the Settlement Museum. You can watch me there some time." He smiled. "You can give me a big tip and help me pay my rent."

I chuckled. "I'll do that; I love street performers."

Remy checked his watch. "It was nice meeting you, but I have to run. The city gives us a time slot, and if I'm late, someone else gets my place."

After Remy rushed downstairs, I spent a few minutes straightening up the front unit.

Then I heard something downstairs that sent a shiver through me.

Beachley was barking. Someone was touching my things.

I raced downstairs and found an old woman in a damp raincoat patting Beachley on the head. I instinctively gathered up my belongings while keeping a close eye on her.

"Sorry I'm late, boss!" she said.

Boss? She must be mad as a hatter.

She had a small, bony frame and her silver hair was pinned into a bun. Her glasses, secured by a gold chain around her neck, had lenses so thick they made her eyes look huge and child-like. But what really drew my attention was her bizarre hat featuring a tiny birdcage.

Apart from her loopy headwear, she was closer to the stereotypical image of an old lady than anyone I'd ever seen—except for her clothes, which were tailored and surprisingly youthful.

The old lady held out her hand. "Dorothea Davenport, at your service. You can call me Dottie."

I tried not to look bewildered as I shook it.

Dottie clucked disapprovingly at the skateboard I was holding in my other hand. "Aren't you a little old for that?"

I probably should have left my board at home, or at least added shock pads for a quieter ride over paving stones. But *The Wavester* and I were inseparable. I wouldn't dream of travelling without it.

"Naw, it's the next best thing to surfing," I replied. "I almost brought my surfboard as a souvenir, but I figured I'd look stupid."

"You don't strike me as someone who worries about that."

Before I could compose myself enough to reply, a kettle whistled in the break room. Dottie's eyes grew wider than they already were, and she rubbed her hands together. "That's our coffee. I thought you might enjoy a cup while we discuss my employment!"

She dashed into the kitchen with surprising speed. A moment later, I heard dishes clattering.

"Just a moment," I protested, following her into the kitchen. "I still don't know who you are, and I don't know where you got the idea I'm hiring. I've only been in town a few hours."

Dottie didn't seem to hear me. She pulled two mugs from the cupboard and spoons from a drawer. I wondered how she knew her way around my kitchen. Had she been there before? Was she a ghost? If wrinkles were anything like tree-stump rings, I'd place her age at around three hundred.

For all I knew, she could have been the original owner.

Dottie placed our mugs on the wooden table along with a glass carafe of steaming black coffee. "I ground it myself this morning," she said, holding up a clear bag of coffee. "It's my own special breakfast blend of five beans."

It smelled delicious, and I hadn't enjoyed a good cup of java in days. "I'd never turn down coffee or a friendly conversation, but I'm really not hiring."

Dottie removed her glasses, unpinned and shook out her long hair, then removed her white gloves one finger at a time while sizing me up from across the table. "It's my age, isn't it? All you see is an old lady. But I'll have you know I'm a hard worker, and I'm still sharp as a tack."

I laughed. "You're persistent, I'll give you that. Why don't you pour us some of that coffee and we'll start there. I have some tarts from Crème de la Crêpe that I've been dying to try, so you and your magic beans couldn't have come at a better time."

Dottie smiled and squeezed the plunger to separate the coffee grounds from the liquid, then poured us each a cup. She said, "I'm surprised to see you with such a large box of tarts. They're very high in calories. You look like a man who frets over carbohydrates."

"Oh I do," I said, placing a tart in front of each of us. "You can't be munching all day long and stay in shape for surfing. But I want to sample everything the city has to offer, so I guess you could say I'm on vacation from healthy eating for a while."

Dottie held up her cup. "To clean living."

"To new friends," I toasted.

We clinked our mugs together and drank. The coffee was full-bodied, rich, and exotic.

Before I'd even consider offering her a job, I needed to know more about her than her name and the fact she could brew a perfect cup of coffee, but it was certainly a good start. I closed my eyes and imagined sun-wrinkled Costa Rican coffee pickers, floating dream-like through rows of coffee trees, lovingly collecting the red berries just for me.

I leaned back in my chair and put my feet up.

"Don't you own any socks?" Dottie asked with a disgusted look.

"Sure, plenty. They're back home in Vancouver."

"So what's your obsession with surfing, anyway?"

"Oh, man, don't get me started." I grinned. "There's nothing as exhilarating as being spit out the back of a blue barrel. One righteous tube ride is worth a lifetime of meditation. You should try it some time."

She narrowed her eyes and stared at me without speaking.

I took a bite of my sour lemon tart and washed it down with a gulp of hot coffee. What could be more sublime? *Two tarts,* I supposed. Too bad the old lady was eating my other one. But no matter, I could always go back for more, and check in on my new friend Sophie.

"This coffee is the best I've ever had, Dottie. A buddy of mine has one of those single-cup coffee makers, but this is much better."

Dottie nodded in agreement. "Those new coffee makers are convenient, but nothing beats a simple coffee press and fresh-ground beans."

"I'm not a big fan of technology," I said.

"Me either. Don't get me started on cell phones with all those bells and whistles."

"I agree—the old stuff usually works just as well, if not better."

Dottie smiled. "The same can be said about people, no?"

I shrugged.

She crammed the rest of her tart into her mouth and pulled a yellowing fragment of newspaper from her purse. I watched tart crumbs bob on her red lipstick while she smoothed the paper on the table and motioned for me to take a look.

A photo in the article showed the front of my building with a large sign above the shop window that read *Quebec in Wax*. Guy and Dottie flanked the mayor, who held a pair of huge novelty scissors to cut the official ribbon.

"We ran this business together for many years," she began, "but it never turned a profit. Guy was driven by money, so gradually he spent less time here and more at his antique store. In the end, this place just died out."

She stared into her coffee for a moment, lost in memories. "Those were the best years of my life. I've often dreamed someone would re-open the business, so when I heard you were coming, I rushed right over. I know I can be a little pushy, but that can be a good quality in sales, wouldn't you say? And I know this business, you could use me."

She looked at me hopefully over the frame of her

glasses while she took a long sip of coffee. When she lowered her mug, the crumbs from the top of her mouth were gone.

"I'd love to have you work here again, Dottie, but I can't afford to make any mistakes. I have three months to turn this place around, starting with the vacation rentals. I'll have to crunch the numbers to see if a gift shop is even worth opening."

She reached across the table and put her wrinkled hand on my arm. "Forget about paying me, at least not with money. I just want to contribute and feel those creative juices again. This place is full of wonderful memories for me, and it would be a hoot to be back. Besides, I have my pension and I make all the money I need creating fascinators."

I raised an eyebrow. "Fascinators? You mean like that thing on your head?"

She looked like she'd been slapped. "This *thing* is a top seller on eBay and Etsy. I make a men's line, too."

I slurped my hot coffee. "Sorry to break it to you, but men aren't going to wear those."

"I have sales that prove otherwise. Men's fascinators are the next big thing. Right now I make gateway hats with sports teams and such on them, just so men can get accustomed to wearing them. Then gradually I'll add flowers and beads. They won't see it coming!"

I always believed that if you want to win in surfing or in business, you need to choose your waves wisely; I knew that I should keep my mouth shut. How had I felt when my dad had ridiculed my methane harvesting business? Or when my friends had laughed at my invention for shoe rakes that I named *Chicken Feet*?

I scanned the article. "What's this about a wax museum? This storefront is barely large enough for retail."

"You didn't know?" Dottie asked, her face brightening. "Well, you're in for a surprise! I'll give you the grand tour. Hurry up and finish that."

I grabbed my mug and tart and gestured for her to lead the way. Feelings of anticipation and curiosity stirred inside me, a sensation I hadn't felt in years.

A grand tour of what? Did I own a wax museum, too?

She led me down a flight of stairs at the back of the gift shop. "It's dark down here, so watch your step."

Most of the light bulbs were flickering or dead, so it took a moment for my eyes to adjust. We stood at the end of a long hallway with stalls containing wax dioramas on each side. A long velvet rope served to keep visitors from touching the exhibits.

Furniture, boxes and junk littered the entire museum. A few of the stalls had even been re-purposed as makeshift storage lockers for the mattresses and furniture of past tenants. Decades of cobwebs and dust draped everything in sight.

Whatever I had expected, this wasn't it. But Dottie was clearly pleased with what she saw. "It's a bit untidy, but all things considered, it's looking good."

"A bit untidy? The Great Pacific Garbage Patch is a bit untidy compared to this."

"Oh, you're all wet," Dottie said with a dismissive wave. "This place cleans up well. You'll see."

She approached the nearest wax figure and leaned across the velvet rope to inspect the clothing. "I made each and every one of these costumes. I was a dressmaker for half of my life and a theatrical costume designer the other half. All the clothes and accessories on these figures are accurate for the age and status of the character, as well as the era."

"What about the furniture and backgrounds and stuff?"

"That was all Guy. He insisted on having full control over the artistic vision of the museum. Unfortunately, he wasn't creative and he loused everything up. Most of the exhibits are just wax figures sitting on crappy furniture from his antique store. If he was feeling whimsical, he might place a candle on a table. But he wasn't whimsical very often."

I walked along the displays. "Who made the wax figures?"

"Guy acquired his first set through his antique business. He knew they'd be hard to resell, but they were antiques created by famous modelers at the world's greatest waxworks. To make a long story short, he had an empty basement here, and he knew that I knew about costumes. The rest is history."

I leaned forward and took a close look at the wax face of Jacques Cartier. The wax gave his skin a true-to-life translucency. I could see tiny pores and follicles in the face, and the glass eyes, lashes and eyebrows were almost indistinguishable from the real thing. In spite of my initial disappointment, my excitement was growing. "Amazing detail. They're so real, it's creepy."

"That's one of the good ones," Dottie said. "For the first few years, this museum was a labor of love for Guy. He ordered new wax figures from catalogues, and each of them cost north of five thousand dollars."

I whistled. "Wow! You'd need a lot of customers to cover that expense."

"That was the problem. When his focus shifted back to his antique business, he started cutting corners and buying cheap plastic figures from China. In the end, he hired students to make figures for him out of wooden forms and plaster, and they look ridiculous."

To make her point, she led me to a figure down the hall. The head and hands were bumpy and cartoon-like.

It looked exactly like what it was: poorly-painted papier-mâché. The body was incorrectly proportioned with short, crooked legs, and a long torso. I'd seen better homemade efforts propped up on porches during Halloween season.

I placed my hands on my hips, taking it all in. This was *my museum*. My mind whirled, processing the possibilities. I could combine the better quality wax figures with home-made lighting and audiovisual effects to bring historic scenes to life, just as I'd done in art school. If I went for quality and not quantity, there was enough there for the start of a decent tourist attraction. I could work on the displays on my own time, and consider it a hobby for now with no real commitment.

It was nutty and financially irresponsible. Heck, opening a wax museum would be financially equivalent to giving ventriloquism lessons. But as a supplementary source of income, it was certainly worth considering.

The museum was a dark maze of hallways. The only light came from spotlights trained on the figures. Dottie led me through the rest of the displays, giving a brief history lesson at each stop. Most figures were of politicians and local celebrities from the early eighties. I thought about how exciting a wax museum would have been prior to television and computers.

Dottie seemed to read my mind. "The role of wax museums has changed a lot since Madame Tussaud in the eighteenth century. Before television, this was how many people would get their news. It was the only way to see what famous people or royalty looked like in full color."

"So a place like this was their idea of fun?" I asked.

"Not exactly," she said dreamily, gliding her hand along the velvet rope. "The original waxworks were nothing like this. They were theatrical spectacles with sound, lights, and special effects. They were designed to entertain and give people a great experience for their money. So you can imagine why there's little interest today in visiting a wax museum like this one."

I followed her to an office/workroom at the far end of the basement. A heavy desk dominated the room, along with sewing machines, bolts of fabric, boxes filled with fiberglass arms and legs, and prosthetic eyes. Plus some unrecognizable devices that I assumed were involved in the production of wax figures.

"I guess this is where all the magic happened," I said.

Dottie inspected her sewing machine. "Yes, I used to spend a lot of time down here."

Once again, my head was spinning from the possibilities. I sat behind the desk gazing around the room. This was the first time in years that I'd felt stoked about anything, and I knew it was futile to try to talk myself out of it. "Every instinct is telling me to focus on the gift shop and vacation rentals. But I *could* spend a little time on the museum each day," I mused out loud. "We could start with a few exhibits and open up more of the museum over time. We could sell candles shaped like famous people, shirts, and maybe sell books and movies with a wax museum theme."

Dottie bristled with excitement. "I notice you said *we*. So does this mean I'm hired? We're going to re-launch the museum and gift shop?"

When she spoke the words, it seemed so final that I wondered if I was being too reckless. Business school placed a lot of importance on resumes and skill sets, so I knew that I should conduct a formal job interview, and maybe ask Guy if he'd recommend her. But this wasn't Chrysler, and I wasn't paying her anything. My own—as yet untested—business philosophy was that you should hire talented people that you enjoy spending time with.

And that was Dottie.

She sensed my hesitation and sighed. "I'm sorry, Paul, I pushed too hard. The truth is, it's going to be a lot of work. There are no guarantees. Are you sure you're up for it?"

It was too late; the museum had me in her mystical clutch, and it would be impossible to talk me out of it. I placed a hand on Dottie's shoulder, preparing her for my first jewel of wisdom. "Nothing is certain in life. You can be riding the perfect wave one second, and then in the next, it can close out and crumble into white water."

Dottie breathed deeply and stared into the distance. I could tell she was biting her tongue.

I grinned. "Do you want to get started now, or wait until tomorrow?"

"I've been waiting for over twenty years. Right now is perfect."

Dottie swept and filled garbage bags while I collected the larger junk and furniture, sorting them into piles. Every so often we'd perk ourselves up with coffee, and Beachley would get a few minutes outside.

When I finally checked my watch, I was shocked that the whole day had passed. "I'm exhausted. I didn't realize how long we'd been down here."

"That's what happens when you don't have any windows," Dottie said.

I surveyed the room. With the aisles clear, it actually looked like a museum, at least as long as you didn't look too closely at the exhibits. "I'm impressed, Dottie, you're a hard worker."

Dottie stood taller and smiled. "I'm not one to fiddle-faddle around. You did a decent job too." She put on her purse and her gloves. "I suppose I should toddle along and go make dinner for my granddaughter."

"Okay, let's pick this up tomorrow. Now that it's all cleaned up, we can start creating some cool new displays using the best figures and costumes. I'll do some research tonight."

After seeing Dottie off and closing up the museum, Beachley and I went upstairs and claimed the small room with a street view for our own. It made good business sense to leave the larger rooms for families.

I fired up my laptop, flicked on my bedside table lamp and got comfortable in the sack.

My first task was to order a cash system for the store. I liked the system Guy used at Tremblay Antiques: it came with a computer terminal and a cash register, so everything should work well together. And I'd only have one company to deal with for support. Before submitting my order, I added an expensive wide-format printer that I'd use for creating posters and backdrops. My heart sank when I saw the final price tag. With my purchases and taxes, I'd already blown a huge share of my start-up budget. But, I reasoned with myself, it had to be done. You have to spend money to make money.

With the big purchases made, it was time to tackle the research for my museum. I downloaded and skimmed through several books on life as a Quebec settler, taking three pages of notes on everything from home furnishings to the juicy details of their personal interactions. I saved the best book for last—a compendium of sensational events in Canadian history. After an engrossing hour sifting through famous disasters, mysteries, and crimes, it was obvious that I'd never run out of inspiration.

I had a few candidates for my first shocking display: a ghoulish scene portraying Étienne Brûlé being eaten alive by Indians, or one of Jean Duval, the famous traitor whose head was removed and mounted on a pole. Or I could do a family-friendly scene of Cartier's men dying of scurvy, only to be saved by an Iroquois remedy.

But the most engaging story I found was of Marie de La Tour, who took charge while her husband was away, bravely defending fort La Tour with only a small force of men.

I put aside my laptop and notepad and switched off my side table lamp. I needed to remove as many sensory distractions as possible to vividly imagine the scene. Visualization was a technique I'd often used in art school. The trick would be to keep myself awake, especially while lying in a comfy bed with raindrops drumming on the window pane.

In my mind's eye, Marie stood on the battlements of a looming tower. She held her sword high and let loose a defiant war cry, her long black hair buffeted by the winds of cannon fire. But no! It would be better to portray the tragic ending, when she surrenders the tower in exchange for the lives of her men, but is then double-crossed and forced to watch while they're all strangled...

The acrid cannon smoke surrounded me as I climbed, and the artillery blasts pounded my chest like a bass drum in a death metal band. I flattened myself against the tower, pushing myself up from shallow footholds, my fingers groping the slick stones for cracks.

The sulphurous smoke burned my lungs and stung my eyes, but there was a hint of something else in the air...

Something delicious.

I squinted upward through the sweat and tears. Did my eyes deceive me, or had the parapet of the tower become a crêpe station?

Sophie smiled down at me, waving with one hand and holding a coffee pot in the other. I climbed with a new sense of urgency, until I finally pulled myself onto the roof.

Sophie had her back turned to me and was wearing a white bonnet. I touched her on the shoulder. "Sophie! Am I glad to see you..."

When the figure spun around, I realized to my horror that it was actually Todd wearing a hairnet.

I felt the world collapsing around me. I grabbed the ends of his tie and started to choke him, while he sputtered, "Tee-off—is—in—ten—minutes."

Soldiers began to shout and pound on the door to the roof.

I woke up, shaking and disoriented, with Beachley staring at me from the foot of my bed.

The shouting and pounding hadn't subsided with my dream. They were real.

And worse, they were coming from the street just outside my window.

Chapter 3

Drunken tourists. That was the logical explanation. But my bedside clock indicated that I'd slept through the entire night, which surprised me since I was usually a light sleeper and was still on west coast time.

The shouting and banging got louder.

Prepared to do some yelling of my own, I slid open my window and stuck my head out into the cool morning air. The sun was just creeping over the horizon, streaking the abandoned blue-grey streets with golden light.

Across the street, a man was hammering his fist on the door to Tremblay Antiques and shouting at someone inside to stop what he was doing. He alternated between yanking on the handle and pressing his face against the glass.

Was there an accident? Had Guy had a heart attack? The cobwebs of sleep were quickly wrenched from my mind and replaced with alarm. I threw on some clothes and rushed down the stairs and out my front door.

The man in front of the antique store had a bushy moustache and curly hair, styled into an old-school mullet, and he wore a rumpled security guard uniform. By the time I reached the street he'd stopped yelling. His arm was drawn back, preparing to smash the glass with a dark pipe.

"Hey! Just a—" I began to call out.

The glass door exploded into a million sparkling shards. I stopped running and instinctively turned my head to protect my eyes. When the deafening crashing subsided, I looked up to see the man reach through the security bars and let himself in. I was right on his heels when he ran into the store and knelt next to Guy's motionless body.

The man finally noticed me when he heard my footsteps behind him. "He's been attacked! Someone just ran to the back of the store," he shouted. "I'll call the police, don't let him get away!"

Acting purely on reflex, I took off like an adrenaline-fuelled rocket, quickly and systematically searching the rabbit warren of aisles and merchandise, in case Guy's attacker was hiding in the store.

When I reached the rear door, I pushed on the latch bar to open it, using the fabric of my shirt to avoid smearing any fingerprints that the assailant might have left.

The back alley was silent and deserted.

There was nothing but parked cars, garbage bins, and fences. An agitated dog began barking in one of the apartment windows that overlook the alley. If someone had come out this door before me, he must have done it very quietly.

I caught the steel door just before it slammed shut behind me. It was a heavy self-locking model with a security keypad mounted on the outside. I was familiar with these doors from my rebellious youth. My friends and I would wait in the alley behind the local movie theatre until somebody left, then we'd catch the door before it closed and sneak inside for the next showing.

I slipped back inside and headed to the front of the store to check on Guy, hoping desperately that he was more alive than he appeared. I'd hate to have to convey the bad news to my parents on my very first morning in town, as they might think I was involved, if only in some negligent or roundabout way. And the last thing I wanted was for them to cancel our deal.

When I passed Guy's office, I heard a coffeemaker sputtering at the end of its brewing cycle. I stopped and looked inside. The computer was turned on, and a rain jacket hung on the back of his chair. Something didn't add up, but I couldn't put my finger on it.

The front door was locked, and the back door had no outside handle. So there were only two possible ways that the attacker could have entered: he either followed Guy inside through the back door, or Guy let him in through the front door and then immediately relocked it.

The first option seemed unlikely. First, the back door closed itself too quickly for someone to slip in unnoticed—certainly my friends and I could never manage it when we sneaked into movies. And if someone did slip in, they would have attacked Guy before he'd had a chance to make coffee and turn on his computer.

This meant that either the attacker had his own key to the store, or Guy had invited him inside and started the coffee. Sophie had mentioned that Guy bought his coffee at the crêperie every morning, so it stood to reason that he wouldn't be using his own coffee maker unless he had a guest.

So the question was, why had a presumably friendly visit end in violence?

I returned to the front of the store and surveyed the scene.

Next to Guy's body laid a heavy iron bar, with stubby legs on one end and a ball on the other. Dark blood had pooled beneath Guy's head. I fought back a wave of nausea. I didn't need a medical degree to diagnose his condition.

The man with the mullet slipped a phone in his pocket and turned to me. "He's dead. Did you get a look at the killer?"

I stared at Guy's body, unable to reply. It was odd to see someone alive one day and dead the next. He was wearing another novelty T-shirt. This time it read *Born to Pick*. His hand clutched a carved walking stick with a bicycle horn attached to it.

I wish I'd had more time to get to know him; he'd seemed like such a cool old dude.

"Did you see the killer?" the man repeated.

"No, I didn't see anybody. I even checked the alley. Who are you?"

"I'm Bernard Curtius." The man stifled a yawn with the back of a dirty looking hand. "Sorry, I probably look as bad as I feel— just got off work. Too bad we didn't get here a few minutes earlier."

The whoop of a police siren grabbed my attention, and then bright lights from a squad car reflected around the store. Several uniformed officers rushed in, while another patrol officer remained outside and began stretching crime tape around the sidewalk.

A tall grey-haired man with an athletic build began barking orders. "Everyone, stay right where you are! My name is Detective Landry. Who placed the call?"

"I did," Bernard said. "The suspect fled through the back door. The victim is Guy Tremblay, the owner of this store. Looks like he was murdered during the course of a robbery."

Landry smiled when he saw Bernard. "Can't stay away from crime scenes, eh? A year off the force and here you are, like a moth to the flame. What's the matter—being a security guard doesn't do it for you anymore?"

Bernard chuckled and shook the detective's hand. "How the hell are you, Landry? Any chance I get to be a pain in your ass, I take it."

I was annoyed by the detective's and Bernard's breezy banter. I'd taken an instant liking to Guy; he was an old friend of my family and seemed like he shouldn't have an enemy in the world. But the presence of his dead body at their feet didn't seem to dampen their mood in the least. I'd had a dislike of authority for as long as I could remember, so I wasn't really surprised.

"If you guys are done catching up," I said coldly, "Why don't you try catching the killer before he gets away?"

Detective Landry froze, turning to me with a frosty look. "I've got a better idea. How about you stand there and shut your mouth, princess?"

I'd never been able to keep my mouth shut, which is one of the reasons I was suspended from school so often. Fortunately, surfing managed to mellow me out enough to get my life together. My dad would have disagreed, of course. He insisted that hanging out with my sketchy beach friends was the root of all my problems.

I bristled at him calling me *princess*. No doubt he was jealous of my long and lustrous hair.

Landry returned his attention to Bernard, flipped open his police log and turned to a blank page. "So give me the rundown. I can't wait to hear the part where you got mixed up in this."

Bernard adopted the official tone commonly used in law enforcement. "At six-thirty, I was passing by and heard sounds of a struggle. Through the window, I saw the victim lying motionless on the floor. Somebody in a dark trench coat was fleeing the scene toward the rear of the store. I shouted and banged on the door, hoping to either rouse the victim or get the assailant to turn around so I could see his face. I then used my nightstick to break the glass and gain access to the property. I checked for vital signs and confirmed the victim was dead. This other gentleman," he said, gesturing my way, "followed me into the store and gave chase. The assailant must have escaped through the back door."

"That all?" Landry asked.

"Yup."

When the crime scene photographer finished snapping pictures, Landry squatted down for a closer look at the murder weapon. With a poor impression of a Cockney accent, he asked, "This the bar what done him in, guv'nor?"

He was trying to push my buttons, which wasn't hard since I had more buttons than an elevator in a five star hotel. I'd been mocked, hassled, and occasionally pepper sprayed by the local barneys for years, so it took everything in me to stay calm. But I'd promised my parents before I'd left that I would be respectful, and I was determined to keep that promise even if it wasn't reciprocated.

"This man," I said evenly, gesturing at Guy, "is a friend of my family. I think you should try and show a little respect."

To his credit, Landry winced and his demeanor softened. He put his hand on my shoulder and said, "I apologize; that was unprofessional. Making jokes is how some of us deal with stress. Sometimes we cross the line."

I stepped back and crossed my arms, resolving to keep silent and let them continue with their work. With any luck, they'd soon let me leave, or at least cover up Guy's body so that I wouldn't have to look at it again.

"I'm sure he understands," Bernard said, sending me a friendly wink. "But yes, that's what's *done him in*. A solid bronze andiron with a cannonball finial. Very formal design. Circa 1970."

Landry inspected the price tag and whistled. "And very expensive. Five thousand dollars! This killer had taste."

A female officer approached to have a look over

Landry's shoulder. Furrowing her brows, she asked, "Why wouldn't he take it with him? The price was right on it."

Landry said, "It's hard to move something like this on the black market. Besides, would you want to run with this thing?" He weighed it in his hand. "It's got to be at least twenty pounds. Maybe he found something lighter and more valuable. But good luck figuring out what it was in this golden emporium."

"So you think robbery was the intent, and the victim walked in on him?" the female officer asked.

"I think so. If murder was the primary motive, he would have brought his own weapon. I'd say this was not premeditated murder. There's a lot of expensive stuff in here. It's almost a foregone conclusion that Mr. Tremblay would get robbed at some point."

"Take a look at this," Bernard said, pointing at the storage cabinets under the sales counter. A decorative sword lay on the floor near his feet. "Looks like the thief pried open the drawers with a sword."

Landry signaled one of the officers to check it out, and I craned my neck around him to take a look too. Landry scowled at me. "What do you think this is, a murder mystery dinner? Get back. I'm not gonna say it again."

He turned his attention back to Guy's body, where a pair of officers were collecting blood and hair samples. Another officer used a tiny vacuum on his clothing, collecting microscopic clues from the crime scene.

The detective approached me and flipped to a new page in his book. "Now it's your turn. Who are you, and what exactly is your relationship to the deceased?"

Before I could answer, Napoleon stormed through the front door and headed our way. He pointed at me, his face red with anger. I could hear the air rush through his crooked nose as his chest heaved. "Paul Wainscott did this!"

He swung his gaze to the detective. "He killed Guy!"

Chapter 4

Everyone stopped what they were doing and turned first to Napoleon, then to me.

"He just came here yesterday, and now Guy's dead," Napoleon said. "I overheard Guy telling him about all the valuables in the store. And just look at his long hair and tattoos. He's probably a drug addict."

The young officer who followed Napoleon inside, caught him by the arm and ushered him back to the front door. "Sorry, sir. I was taking his statement and he got away from me. This is Napoleon Roy, the co-owner of the store."

Landry sighed. "We've met. Napoleon, go home. I'll call you when we're through here. You won't be opening today."

Landry turned to me with a weary smile. "If he had his way, everyone who isn't Quebecois would be arrested. But you aren't off the hook yet. I have a few questions." He thumbed through his dog-eared notebook until he found the page he was looking for. "Bernard mentioned that you chased the killer. Tell me about that."

"Bernard saw the killer running to the back of the store, so I ran after him, but I didn't see anybody."

"So you let him get away," Landry said, more of a statement than a question.

I tried to ignore whatever implication was embedded into Landry's words. I paused, wondering how many of my own theories to disclose. "I noticed Guy had made coffee, which is weird because the girl in the crêperie next door said he always buys his coffee there. Oh, and don't worry, I was careful not to leave any prints."

Detective Landry's pencil stopped. He raised an eyebrow at me and smirked. "Let me guess—CSI fan? Nowadays everyone wants to be a detective. Even Bernard Curtius here wants to open his own detective agency."

A nearby officer chuckled.

Landry added, "My wife lives for that stuff. They should make *CSI: Quebec*. Nothing would happen, though. Nothing ever happens here. Lowest crime rate in North America." He paused and looked me dead in the eye. "Until you got here, that is."

I shrugged. So much for trying to help.

Landry resumed the interview. "So what's your relationship to the deceased?"

"An old friend of the family. I only met him once, about twenty years ago. He met my family when we rented the place across the street. He just sold me the building."

"Got it." Landry put away his notebook and pen.

"So what happens next?" I asked.

"Well, I'm going home to enjoy a nice pipe of tobacco and curl up in bed with Charles Dickens. What do you think happens next? I'm going to investigate. I know where to find you if I need you."

With that, he turned to his fellow officers, and I was dismissed.

I returned home in a daze.

Beachley was waiting for me at the door with her tail wagging, so I took her for a walk around the block to clear my head.

Did Guy have any family that should be notified? He'd mentioned an ex-wife, so I assumed the police would get in touch with her to sort everything out. Then, of course, there was Dottie, his old friend. They weren't as close as they once were, but surely the news would be devastating to her. I'd also need to call my parents. Apparently they were friends of Guy's, too.

It was still early when I returned, and I didn't expect Dottie for a few more hours.

Figuring work would be a good distraction, I tackled the gift shop with my full energy and attention. The opening of the wax museum was high on the list and could net strong returns in the long-term, but the gift shop would be my best chance of making some money in the short-term.

At the very least, I'd like to be open before the New France Festival. I could take advantage of all the foot traffic to get a mailing list going, and then I could send out updates when the museum opened. But who knew? With Dottie's help, I might be able to get part of the museum ready in time, too.

I went to the break room and put the kettle on.

Beachley headed straight for the rug in front of the fireplace and curled up. I was a big fan of fireplaces myself, especially the wood-burning variety. They were three times better than gas, since burning wood was not only warm, but it sounded and smelled nice too.

"Aren't you forgetting something, Beachley?" I said.

I put out fresh water and a scoop of food, and she sprang to her feet, scrambling towards it in a frenzy. "Whoa, careful. You're going to wipe out."

After sampling the great food in this city, I knew exactly how Beachley felt. If I saw one of Sophie's ham and cheese crêpes right now, I'd respond the same way. I'd had an unusually big appetite since I arrived, and the morning's excitement had made me ravenous.

If it weren't for Guy's murder, I'd have gone across the street for breakfast. But in a small community like this, there would be a lot of excited chatter and gossip in the crêperie right now, and I couldn't deal with it.

Just as I poured the boiling water over Dottie's special coffee blend, I heard a tapping at the front door.

It was Dottie. She had her nose pressed to the glass and looked upset. I ushered her out of the rain and into the kitchen.

"Did you hear? Oh, it's terrible," she said. "I heard sirens this morning and found out there'd been an accident at the antique store. Guy is dead! Did you see anything?"

"I'm afraid it was no accident," I said with a grimace. "He was murdered. And yes, I was there."

"Murder? It's like a bad dream. Who on earth would want to harm that dear man?"

I was wondering the same thing, and was tempted to ask her what she knew about his family and business dealings. But that would have to wait. I helped her into a chair instead. "They think it happened during a robbery. Let's both try and relax for a bit, and we'll talk about this later."

"Yes, I think that would be best. It's just a shock to imagine him gone." She took a deep breath and shook herself, making an obvious effort to get past her shock. "That coffee smells great. Just what I need to calm my nerves."

I poured us each a cup and spooned sugar into mine.

Dottie set a takeout bag on the table. "I figured you didn't eat yet, so I stopped to get us breakfast. Nothing fancy—just egg muffins and hash browns."

"You eat fast food? You're so authentically French, I expected a Croque Monsieur or something. I guess that's a cliché."

Dottie just hunched over her sandwich and bit into it. She was distracted and not in the mood for light conversation. I was feeling bummed out, too.

"Thank you," I said. "I appreciate it."

We finished our meal in silence. By the time I'd cleared the table, Dottie seemed more like her old self again. I was impressed by her resilience. I'd only known Guy for one day, and I felt terrible. I couldn't imagine how Dottie felt after knowing him for decades.

Dottie smiled at me, but I sensed a fierce resolve beneath the surface. "I'm feeling a little better now. I'm ready to hear everything you know about Guy's murder."

I refilled our coffees, then related the morning's events to her in detail, leaving nothing out except the sight of Guy's lifeless body. I wished I could get that image out of my head, so I wasn't about to put it in hers.

Dottie didn't have much to say. She sat quietly, taking it all in, and we had a moment of silence after my story was done. Finally, she said, "Maybe we'll feel better after some hard work."

"Agreed." I took out the list of ideas that I'd jotted down the night before. "First of all, I think entertainment should come first. History can be pretty dry stuff. If we fill the whole museum with boring displays, nobody will come. I want to bring showmanship back, in the style of P.T. Barnum and Madame Tussaud's."

"It sounds exciting," Dottie said, "but if you're talking about animatronics and special effects, that can be very, very expensive."

"Well, I'm not ruling anything out yet, but my goal is to make the museum fun without spending a lot of money. I learned how to build amazing art installations at school for next to nothing. You'd be surprised how many corners you can cut with a little creativity. Trust me, if we can imagine it, I can build it. Cheap."

Dottie looked impressed. "Did you have anything in

mind?"

"Sure do. First, I know everyone's going to expect to see Celine Dion and Rocket Richard. Forget about them," I said. "Bo-ring. Let's give them something they haven't seen before and won't see anywhere else. Terrible and fascinating scenes from history, brought to life by your costumes and my special effects."

"It sounds exciting!" Dottie said, "Like the great wax museums of the past. Maybe we can even create special temporary exhibits depicting things in the news. It would give us an excuse to send out an email blast and get people to come back."

I laughed. "An email blast? Where did you pick up that term? Awesome idea, though."

"Thanks," Dottie said. "I can't tell you how great it feels to be doing this again. It makes an old woman feel worthwhile. So what's our first exhibit?"

"I have a list of ideas, but why don't we start with something that has impact, and set the tone for the new museum? Have you heard of Étienne Brûlé?"

"Of course! He was an interesting fellow, wasn't he? He was a traitor to Quebec and was tortured and eaten by the Huron Indians."

"Right. He was also an outlaw who violated every taboo you can imagine. I'll have a lot of good material to work with."

"Okay, boss," Dottie said, saluting. "I think we already have the perfect costume for Étienne. Just let me know who else will be in the scene, and I'll take care of them, too. Oh, and speaking of French history, you'll need to rent a costume for yourself for the New France Festival. I suggest you go down to Old Fashion today before the good ones are gone."

"Why do I have to dress up?" I asked.

"Everyone does, including many tourists. As a merchant, it's expected of you. Go and see Francine today—she runs the place. She's also a friend of your tenant, Remy."

"It sounds like this festival is a big deal around here," I said.

"Oh, yes, and it gets busier every year. There are street performers, concerts, and lots of food. If you dress up, you get to take part in the big parade, too. I won't spoil the surprise and tell you too much—you'll just have to wait and see."

"I'm sold. I'll pay Francine a visit after lunch."

Dottie said, "Put some socks on before you go, for heaven's sake."

"Okay, I'll buy some socks."

"And don't bore her with talk about blue barrels and other nonsense."

"Yes, Dottie."

I put our cups in the sink, and we moved to the empty store. Dottie surveyed the room with a concerned look on her face. "Well, I hope you have money coming out the wazoo, because it'll cost a fortune to stock these shelves. You'll need large minimum orders to get wholesale prices."

I followed her gaze. "Nothing in my wazoo, I'm afraid. But I do have a little cash set aside. Why don't we start by selling things from other shops around here, on consignment? We can cherry pick the products we want that fit our theme. Later, we can start ordering our own merchandise for a better margin."

"That's not a bad idea," Dottie said. "I know all the merchants around here. We could reach out to local artists, too." She paused and stared at the sales counter. "What are we going to use for a cash register? I've got a metal box at home I could bring in."

"Already taken care of. I ordered a super deluxe point-of-sale system. I'm cheap, but I don't skimp where it counts."

"I'm so glad to hear it," Dottie said. "I'm an old-fashioned gal, but when it comes to accounting systems, I prefer the latest and greatest. It makes your life so much easier."

"Great minds think alike," I said. "Let's start by giving this place a good cleaning, then we can start contacting merchants and filling our shelves over the next few days."

We put in a few solid hours of work. Dottie scrubbed the floors until they shined, while I cleaned the windows, shelves and sales counter. When we stopped to admire our work, my stomach growled so loud even Dottie heard it.

"What do you say we grab some lunch at Crème de la Crêpe?" she asked. "My treat."

"Thanks for the offer, but I'm going to head over to Old Fashion now. I'll grab some street eats after that."

"Suit yourself. I'll just finish up here and call it a day. I've got some errands to run, but I'll be back first thing tomorrow."

Since Dottie figured I should get spiffed up, I went upstairs and checked myself out in the mirror. I was wearing sandals, a pair of cut-off jean shorts, and a faded surfing T-shirt. My hair was messy, and I had a two day beard, giving me the overall look of a hung-over carnival worker.

Even though I liked what I saw, I knew I had to clean up my image if I wanted other merchants to take me seriously. I quickly shaved and brushed my hair, then threw on a white button-down shirt. When I took another look at my reflection, I was surprised by how much I resembled my father, and it occurred to me that he might have looked into the very same mirror during my childhood vacation. Maybe I'd ask him some time.

For now, I was ready to roll.

Chapter 5

It turned out that Old Fashion was just down the street. It seemed everything you needed in this tight-knit community was within walking distance. I wondered if I'd ever need to drive my awesome van again.

The sales clerk was helping a young couple pick out a costume. She looked like a gypsy with olive skin, curly hair and thick, trendy glasses. "I'll be right with you," she called out to me cheerfully.

I took the opportunity to browse. They had racks of period clothing suitable for use at fairs and Renaissance festivals. All of it was high-quality stuff, and judging from the mannequins, very fashionable, too. Besides the typical puffy shirts, knee-length pants and dresses, there were all the boots, wigs and accessories you'd ever need—and then some. They even had some items tending toward the risqué—things with bustiers and lace. I had to admit I wouldn't mind seeing some of those items in the big parade.

The back of the store was filled with merchandise I assumed was there to increase revenue during non-festival months: decorative swords, ornate chess boards, and, of course, the all-pervasive mugs and souvenirs. Many of the shops seemed to use the same supplier. I made a mental note to avoid using them.

The sales clerk finished ringing up her customers and greeted me with a smile that lit up her face. I noticed the name tag just above her low-cut Renaissance bodice, which left little to the imagination.

"You must be Francine?" I said, forcing my eyes back up.

"Busted," she said.

Interesting choice of words, I thought.

"I'm Francine Chapelle. What can I do for you?" she asked.

"I'm Paul Wainscott. I just moved here, and I've been told I need a costume for the festival. A friend gave me your name."

Her eyes narrowed. "One day in Quebec and already you have friends? Is it because of your rock-star looks or your personality?"

"I'd like to think it's a little of both," I grinned back.

She tapped her finger on the counter while she scrutinized my physique. "Most guys just wear a puffy shirt, knee-length pants, long socks, and a three-cornered hat. But I'm working on a new costume that not a lot of men could pull off. You'd have to be in great shape and crave attention. Most of all, you'd have to be secure in your masculinity. So let me ask you—" She leaned in closer. "Are you secure in your masculinity?"

I could smell her perfume. "Quite the opposite. I'm always looking for new ways to toughen up my image. Why do you think I went to art school and grew out my hair?" I flipped my hair back for emphasis.

"I like my guys to have long hair. Are you in a band?"

"What do you think?" I asked, breaking into a head-banging air-guitar solo.

"I'll take that as a no."

After a good laugh, she said, "Seriously though, this would be the perfect costume for you if you're interested. It's made with the finest material: embroidered vest, golden ribbons, silk stockings, and a powdered wig. A lot of guys would be afraid of looking like a dandy. But I think you would rock it."

"It sounds great, but I'm on a tight budget."

"I'll tell you what—I'll give you the friends and family rate. The truth is, I was just planning on using it as a window display. Buy me dinner some time and we'll call it even. Your choice of restaurant."

"Sweet deal," I said, pumping my fist. "I really appreciate it. So do you own this shop then?"

"Unfortunately not. I couldn't afford the rent. I just manage it. The owners are at the main location in Montreal. I do have my own business, though. I give lantern ghost tours at night." She rolled her eyes and smiled. "Imagine that—earning a four-year degree in history to give ghost tours."

"I think you're lucky," I said cheerfully. "You work in a beautiful city and meet interesting people like me every day. You run your own business and get to teach people about history. Look at me, I'm chucking my old life away to run a wax museum with almost no hope of supporting myself. It's crazy, but I've never felt so alive."

Francine seemed surprised by what she heard. "You bought the gift shop across from Tremblay Antiques? The creepy wax museum?"

"That's the one. And thanks for coming up with a great slogan for it." I laughed. "But I know what you're going to say. Your friend Remy St. Claire lives in my building—he mentioned you know each other."

Her face clouded. "How did Remy look? He's been acting strange lately. I'm worried that he might be getting into mischief again. I call him *Dummy* because he has no common sense, but I told him it was because he stands still for a living. Yesterday, he seemed on top of the world, but today he seemed nervous."

"I didn't see him today, but he seemed to be in good spirits yesterday. Maybe he was upset by Guy's murder?"

Francine gasped. "Oh, right! I almost forgot about that. Well, maybe that's it." Her face brightened again. "I see why you're so good at making friends, Paul. I hope you have room for one more."

"Absolutely." I paused, not sure how to proceed. We'd started with costumes, touched on murder, and all I wanted to do was ask her about the wax museum. "Speaking of the museum, I'm looking for unique historical items to stock my shelves. Do you offer wholesale pricing?"

"No," she said, wincing. Then her face brightened. "But you can sell some of our products on consignment if you like. In fact, you can take some things with you right now. I can stop by later and discuss the pricing."

"Terrific! And after you stop by, I can buy you that dinner."

Francine disappeared into the storage room for a few minutes and returned with two file boxes full of clothing, games, and pewter figurines. "I wrote a list of what's in the boxes, but you can verify it if you like."

"Naw, I'm sure it's perfect. And thanks again."

"No problemo. I'll have your costume ready by the weekend."

Then, without warning, she stepped forward and put her arms around my waist. Surprised, I gave her an awkward hug, then realized with horror that she was holding a measuring tape. I felt myself turn red, but Francine acted like nothing happened when she pulled away. In a way, that made it worse.

I noticed a hint of a smile on her face as she squatted down to measure my inseam. Just then, the door chime announced the arrival of a large tour group.

"Well, back to work," she sighed, jotting something down on the back of a business card. This is my number. It was nice meeting you, Paul Wainscott."

"Same here. I'm looking forward to dinner." I pocketed the card and gave her a friendly wave as I left.

I dropped Francine's boxes and Beachley off at home.

Dottie wouldn't be back this afternoon, so it was a perfect time to explore the city. I wanted to check out the other shops, too, and tying up the dog every few minutes would slow me down.

I followed the crowds to the bustling center of the old city, stopping occasionally to pick up supplies for my apartment and museum. The main square was filled with tourists, and more arrived by the minute in tour buses. A throng of people surrounded street performers who stood on tall, square pedestals. I walked over for a closer look, and discovered that one of the performers was my boarder, Remy St. Claire.

Chapter 6

Remy wasn't wearing his bronze sculpture outfit. This time, he was a dressed as a traditional mime with a patchwork hobo costume, white gloves, and a white face. His dark eyebrows and red lipstick really emphasized his expressions, giving him a sarcastic aura.

I had never seen a mime act before. There were no unseen ropes or invisible, confining boxes. Apparently the idea was simply to mimic people, and although I had nobody to compare him too, I could see Remy was quite good at it. His crowd was in hysterics and I had to inch my way forward for a better view.

Somehow he managed to spot me in the crowd. I felt a momentary panic while I waited to see myself reflected in his movements. The crowd laughed when Remy adopted an expression of fear on his face, and nervously wrung an imaginary shopping bag in his hands.

I looked down and realized I was clutching a bag with my recent purchases. This made the crowd laugh even more. I felt myself turn red, and thankfully Remy shifted his attention to a child who'd dropped a handful of coins in his hat.

I left Remy a gigantic tip and headed for a food stand that had bewitched me when I'd passed it earlier. I knew the fat content would be off the charts, but I was irresistibly drawn to the aroma of doughy deep-fried beaver tails. I ordered an apple cinnamon and a chocolate-banana. To complete the meal, a hot chocolate with whipped cream and dark chocolate shavings.

I searched for a place to sit, with a beaver tail in each hand and my hot chocolate perilously wedged under my arm. I sat next to a stone sculpture that looked like Michelangelo's David, seated with his head in his hands, deep in thought. I spread my meal out on the bench, then almost jumped out of my skin when the sculpture cleared its throat and turned to face me. He wordlessly made a shooing gesture with his hand, clearly wanting me to give him a little more space.

"Oops, sorry, bro," I said in English.

"Two dollars fer a picture," he said in a southern drawl. I noticed he was missing a few teeth.

"I didn't bring my camera."

The statue just shrugged and settled back into his pose.

I said, "You're not from around here, I take it?"

He didn't respond. I noticed a bowl between his feet that was painted with a stone texture. There were already a few coins in it, so I tossed in a couple more to keep them company.

He glanced at the bowl when he heard the coins. "Much obliged. To answer yer question, my people are in the mountains of Virginia. Nowadays I ain't got no fixed address."

I sipped my hot chocolate through the fluffy whipped topping, and dabbed my nose with my sleeve. I smiled sheepishly, hoping he didn't notice. "I'm from Vancouver."

He turned to look at me. "I was in them parts a few months back, workin' a ski resort."

I raised both eyebrows and nodded. "Sounds like a lot of fun. Do they have buskers at ski resorts?"

"Naw, I've got other skills," he said with a lopsided smile. "I worked the chair lifts. But I'm glad the season's over. It's right cold workin' outside and I got so 'tard I couldn't see straight. The worse I get doing this is a crick in my back. But like as not, I'll be goin' there again next year."

I handed him one of my beaver tails. "Do you want this? I didn't realize they would be so massive."

I'd known how big they were, of course. I saw other people eating beaver tails near the booth. I ordered two of them because I was a pig, plain and simple.

I don't care," he said with a shrug, taking it from my hands. "But get me one of them hot cocoas next time too." He burst out laughing. "Just messin' with ya."

He bit into his beaver tail, closing his eyes while he savored it. "Mmm, that's right tasty."

"Sounds like an exciting life you lead, with all that travel," I prompted.

"I sure like it. I do a whole circuit. Key West, California, Vancouver, Vegas, and a lot of places besides. I'm fixin' to leave here in a few weeks after the festival is ended."

It occurred to me that this might be an opportunity to learn more about my new tenant, Remy. I bit into my own snack and nodded towards Remy and his big crowd. "He's pretty good, isn't he?"

"Who, Remy? I reckon he's the best."

"So the performers know each other pretty well then?"

He nodded. "Me and him are real good friends. Real good. I helped learn him a new bronze dummy act. I told him it don't mean diddley squat to me if he copies my act, but this here bench is mine. So he performs his dummy act at the bronze fountain across from the Settlement Museum."

I polished off my beaver tail and tossed the paper wrapper into the garbage can next to the bench. "I'm Paul Wainscott," I said, holding out my hand. "I didn't get your name."

"Pleased to make your acquaintance. I'm Cliff Hofstetter." He rubbed his hands together in a futile attempt to clean them, then shook my hand. "Thanks for the treat, buddy."

Beachley was waiting by the door when I returned to the museum. Usually she had a good sense of time and knew when to expect dinner, but today she was almost an hour off. She probably wasn't used to her new surroundings yet. I gave her a scoop of food and put away my groceries and other purchases.

I knew that I shouldn't be using the store and break room as my own personal living space, especially since the expansive plate glass window didn't offer any privacy at night. But I didn't have any tenants yet except for Remy, and I hadn't even had a chance to get properly settled in upstairs.

I spread out all the ingredients to make spaghetti. I knew I couldn't eat out and live on chocolates forever. I rinsed off some dusty pans that I'd found in the cupboard, and began boiling pasta and browning the hamburger. I've never been a big fan of jarred spaghetti sauce, so I'd picked up some spices, tomatoes and tomato paste during my walkabout. I threw it all into a saucepan to simmer.

I figured I might as well organize Francine's merchandise on my shelves while the food cooked.

I arranged the figurines and chess boards on my shelves, spreading them out wide in case I didn't find any more vendors willing to work with me. I cut off the Old Fashion price tags that Francine had attached to them, and replaced them with my own handwritten tags having higher prices. There were also mugs, jewelry and tarot cards. Even though these items didn't feel right for my new store, they were better than nothing for now.

I opened Francine's other file box and found some costumes. On the top there was an exceptionally good quality one for ladies, and one for men. Costumes actually seemed like a good fit for a wax museum gift shop, so I decided to feature them near the window. Knowing there was no shortage of dress forms and mannequins in the basement, I ran downstairs and grabbed two of them for my retail display.

The man's outfit consisted of a waistcoat with long knitted stockings held up by garters. The idea of men wearing garters seemed bizarre to me, but I guessed they were all the rage in the olden days. I set a powdered wig on the plastic head, and a tricorn hat with gold cord and features. From what Francine had told me, this would have been worn by well-to-do guys. A commoner would more likely have worn clothes made from rough woolen fabrics.

The lady mannequin got a gold brocade gown accented with a lace collar and sleeves. I found a pair of gloves and a fan in the box, so I assumed that they were meant for the woman and added them to her outfit.

By the time I had the mannequins fully dressed and positioned where I wanted them, my meal was ready.

I filled a large plate with spaghetti and sauce, and grabbed a beer from the fridge. It felt strange to eat alone in a quiet room in a new town. I was accustomed to eating with the entire family while I was at home, or having pizza with my friends at the beach house where the party never ended. It was a good thing I had Beachley there with me; without her I might have been homesick.

For just a moment I considered bringing my plate upstairs so that I could watch television while I ate, but I'd already wasted too much time today bumming around town. My time would be better spent working if I wanted to turn this business around.

After rushing through the rest of my meal, I washed my dishes and got right back to work.

One of the stops I'd made earlier in the day was to a thrift store. I'd bought a couple of old tape recorders for a few dollars each, as well as some three minute answering-machine cassette tapes that played as an endless loop. My idea was to create some background audio for my first exhibit. If it worked out, I could buy more of the tape players or some old CD players—the thrift store had boxes overflowing with them since they were practically antiques.

I set up my laptop and logged into a website that sold royalty-free music and sound effects. After almost an hour of searching, I bought a dark atmospheric music loop that I thought would set the mood of the Étienne Brûlé exhibit. I also downloaded some audio clips of Indians chanting, leaves blowing, and a crackling fire.

When all of the sound clips were combined into a continuous three-minute audio file, I hooked the microphone jack of the tape recorder into the headphone jack of my laptop and started recording to the cassette. I thought about adding a bilingual voiceover to tell the story of Étienne, but decided against it. Aside from the fact that visitors would speak many different languages, I didn't want to lock into a script. It would be better to print out pamphlets for that. I couldn't wait to let Dottie hear the final result.

I brought the tape machine downstairs to the basement and hid it behind one of the plastic bushes in my exhibit. It was powered by batteries so it would have to be turned on manually for now. But some day I would buy power adapters to plug the machines into the wall. I adjusted the volume and stood back to appreciate my handiwork.

It was, by far, the best sounding empty booth I'd ever seen in a museum.

Since Dottie and I were redoing the exhibits from scratch, I was free to scavenge props and lights from the other displays. I found some backdrops with painted outdoor scenes to cover the walls of the booth, then I dragged in some artificial trees and shrubs. As a finishing touch, I added small clamp-on lights with colored bulbs, positioning them so that they cast an eerie color on the scene.

To complete the tableau, we still needed props and figures depicting Étienne being tortured and eaten. But that was Dottie's job. I was wiped out.

It was time to call it a night.

Chapter 7

I woke to the rumbling of a machine on the street below. Awaking to strange noises was proving to be a major drawback to city living. But at least this morning there was no shouting in the street.

Memories of the crime scene and Guy Tremblay's lifeless body came back to me. A full day had gone by with no news of an arrest, and no contact from Detective Landry or his men. Initially, I feared I'd become their primary suspect, but clearly I wasn't and this concerned me even more. At the very least, I should be a major witness since I was found at the scene of the crime.

Apparently, I would have to do some investigating of my own.

I dragged myself to the window and pushed it open.

Garbage men with orange vests and oversized leather gloves laughed and heaved bags of bottles into a slow-moving truck. It was still raining, and the air was heavy with the scent of wet pavement and baking bread. As a surfer who'd spent most of his life around water, I wasn't particularly bothered by rain, but I missed the sunshine. At least Crème de la Crêpe looked warm; I could already see a few customers sitting in the window booths.

I enjoyed a long hot shower and got ready slowly, taking a few minutes to unpack my bags. I usually left my things in my suitcase when I travelled; I never saw much point in pulling everything out just to put it back again. But I wasn't travelling now. I was home. Maybe unpacking and adding some personal touches to my apartment would help me believe it.

Beachley and I headed downstairs together. When the rain slowed, I directed her to a patch of grass behind the building. A minute later, she was ready to return indoors where she knew food and a fluffy towel waited.

Feeling like a new man, I hastened to the Crêperie with a bounce in my step. It was already the middle of the morning rush, but I lucked out and snagged a primo booth with an unobstructed view of my own building.

As I waited for my waitress, tiny school children wearing uniforms paraded past my window, followed closely by two stern-looking nuns. A refreshing breeze came through the partly-open window. Although it was mid-summer, the mornings in Quebec were still cool enough for a sweater or jacket. I'd made a rookie mistake by packing only tee-shirts.

"Hi, Paul!" Sophie appeared with a welcoming smile and a pot of coffee. She put a mug down in front of me and started to fill it.

"Just half-way," I said. "I've had so much coffee lately I'm getting a Brazilian accent."

Sophie set her pot on the table and slid into the seat across from me, mindless of the other patrons who were waiting to order. "I guess you need it. You've been working long hours over there. I saw the lights on across the street when we closed up."

"Yeah, I'm working like a lunatic but I'm loving every second of it. I like being creative and working with my hands. But I really should spend more time on the guest rooms; they're supposed to pay the bills."

"I'm sure all your rooms will be rented for the festival."

"That's what's so strange," I said intensely. "I found a reservation book that said I was booked right through the summer. Right now every room should be occupied, but there's just me and one other guy."

Sophie twisted her mouth thoughtfully while she watched me add cream to my coffee. Then her face lit up. "Why don't you call the people who made the reservations? That's what I'd do. I'd be like, 'Hey what gives? I've got your bed ready and you're not in it.'"

"That's a great idea! I feel stupid for not thinking of it."

"You should also put up a vacancy sign with your phone number. With the festival coming up, people will be desperate for a place to stay soon."

I raised an eyebrow, took out my phone and started typing. "Just making a note about the vacancy sign on my phone. Thanks for the idea."

"Any time," she said.

Suddenly lost in thought, I clutched my coffee in both hands, basking in its warmth like a bum hunched over a garbage can fire. Sophie looked on with an expression of curiosity, then she leaned in closer to get my attention. "Is everything alright?"

I forced a weak smile. "Sorry, I was thinking about Guy and the antique store. I guess you heard the news?"

"Yep, I'm afraid so. With all the police cars and shouting it was hard to miss. I still can't believe it. Guy was such a big part of life around here. I guess the police think it was a robbery."

I was stunned. "Where did you hear that?"

"Oops." Sophie's eyes popped wide open. "I overheard some police talking while they were here buying coffee. I guess I shouldn't be repeating this stuff."

I shrugged off her concerns while my mind raced. There was no way it was robbery. The facts just didn't fit.

"When Guy came in for his morning coffee, was he acting... strangely?" I asked.

She shook her head. "He didn't show up yesterday. For Guy, that's pretty strange right there."

I humphed and leaned back in my seat, running my hands through my hair. All this investigating was hurting my brain, and, sadly, I no longer had the luxury of a refreshing surf to balance and reset my mind.

After a pause, Sophie said, "I like your tan, by the way."

I was grateful for the topic change. I liked having the Crêperie as a place to relax and forget my problems. And the last thing I wanted to do when spending time with Sophie was talk about murders and business. Even though her advice really was terrific.

"Thanks. I just got back from Honolulu," I replied.

"Really?"

"Nah, not really. I wish."

"So that's how its going to be today?" She grinned. "Well, I was lying too. Your tan is weird. Your hands are darker than your arms."

I spooned brown sugar into my coffee. "It's from wearing a wet suit. I did a lot of surfing back home."

Her eyes grew a fraction wider. "Cool. Are you any good?"

"Slicing waves, that's what I do best."

"All I get to slice around here is toast." Her smile faded. "I actually had a chance to move to Fiji with my parents."

"Seriously? Sounds like there's a story there."

She shrugged and fiddled with my saltshaker. "They run a yoga retreat in Asia now. It's one new adventure after another with them. I swear they're ageing backwards."

"They sound like the coolest parents in the world," I said. Truthfully, I was a bit jealous.

"I guess." She forced a smile and straightened up. "Maybe I'll go to Honolulu myself and try surfing."

"If you dig surfing, you should vaycay in Vancouver with me some time. I'll give you free lessons. You'll need to work on your tan first though. No offense, but next to me you look like a cave fish."

"A cave fish!" she laughed. "Thanks a lot! So what's in it for you if I go?"

"You'd be there to make me look good. Every surfer needs a bunny hanging on his arms. Maybe I'll even let you wax my board."

"Keep dreaming."

"I know you're tempted by the beach life. I've seen you admiring my long sun-kissed hair."

"Ugh. That reminds me, I have to mop out the restrooms."

I laughed and coughed up a mouthful of coffee. "Touché."

"So why all the tattoos?" she asked.

"I guess I went a little overboard in my youth. I wish I hadn't gotten so many. Warn your friends. Tattoos are for idiots."

Sophie's expression darkened. "I have tattoos."

"Really?"

"No, not really," she laughed.

I exhaled. "Oh, man, I thought I really put my foot in my mouth."

"Why do you care so much what I think?"

I hesitated a moment. "I dunno. I guess because I like you."

Easy there, Paul.

"That's sweet; thank you."

"You're welcome." I drained the last of the coffee from my cup. "Seriously though, you shouldn't wait too long to travel. You know what they say, a ball that ceases to roll turns into a square."

Sophie giggled. "Who said that? What does that even mean?"

"Beats me. I was trying to sound wise."

"Well, it worked for about three seconds, until I realized it was nonsense. But the truth is, I'm happy just staying here and living my boring nerd life."

"I'm starting to like it here too," I said.

Sophie jumped to her feet. "I almost forgot, I haven't taken your order yet. Why don't you try a dessert crêpe? They're super good."

"Perfect, I'll take two of them to go. I have to get back to the museum."

A few minutes later, she returned with my order, while balancing plates for other customers in her hands. The morning rush had started, and our long chat had clearly put her behind in her work. She hastily dumped two Styrofoam boxes in front of me, and offered an apologetic smile before disappearing into the crowd.

It was time for me to get back to work, too.

Dottie had already fed Beachley and was boiling water for coffee when I came through the door. She was wearing another one of her crazy hats, and reading a paperback mystery novel at the kitchen table. Whenever she had a free moment and wasn't chatting with me or working, out came one of her whodunits. I'd already seen the cover change twice since we'd met.

"I hope you have a library card," I remarked as I walked in.

She put down her book and smiled. "Oh, don't worry about that. I've got plenty of do-re-mi."

I leaned in for a closer look at her newest fascinator.

Unlike the birdcage hat, this one was actually quite elegant looking, and it depicted a subject matter that was very close to my heart—and my stomach. The hat was shaped like a white saucer with a fluffy ostrich plume. The little cup on the saucer was surrounded by tasty looking chocolates, and white silk flowers stood in for dollops of whipped cream.

"This is just something fun and flirty I made to celebrate the day we met." She stood up and twirled to show it off.

"I like it. You could open your own hat shop."

"Oh, I only do this for fun. They're too labor intensive to be profitable. I just add the money that I make to the kitty, and when I have enough saved up, I'm going to take my granddaughter on a Caribbean cruise. I have six hundred dollars so far."

"Sounds like a blast; I hope you make it."

"What do you mean by that?" she snapped. "You think I might die first?"

Oops. "I meant that life has a way of getting in the way of your plans. And I hope it doesn't; it sounds like a lot of fun."

She visible relaxed. "That's very true, Paul. My late husband and I had dreamt of taking a cruise for thirty years, and just never got around to it. I don't intend on letting that happen this time."

I would've felt bummed out by that, but Dottie's good mood was too contagious.

She noticed my takeout bag and rubbed her hands together. "I'd know that bag anywhere. Did you bring me something to eat?"

"A dessert crêpe. I hope you don't mind sugar for breakfast."

"Not at all. We'll need the energy today; we're going to lug out the old furniture and appliances that we sorted yesterday."

"Ah yes, today's our junk removal day."

The kettle whistled and I prepared our coffee while Dottie set the table with plates and cutlery.

"So," Dottie said, "did you see anything interesting at Old Fashion yesterday?"

"Besides Francine Chapelle? Yeah, she hooked me up. I'm going as a *dandy*."

"You mean a nobleman?"

"Right. Did you get your costume yet?" I asked.

"Oh no, I make my own costumes. I have a whole closet full of them. If I didn't just have the one size, I could start my own rental business like Francine."

"Not to mention, you already have a job," I reminded her with a smile, while pouring our coffees. "Anyway, Francine is worried about her friend Remy. He's been acting pretty nutty lately."

"Remy is the young man who lives upstairs, right?"

"That's that one. He works as a mime. I saw his act yesterday—he's really good!"

Dottie took a bite of her crêpe and had a curious look on her face.

"Something wrong with it?" I asked.

"No, it's delightful. I was just thinking about Remy and Guy's murder. Maybe it's just the storm clouds outside, or maybe I read too many crime novels. But something is afoot. I can feel it."

I nodded thoughtfully. I was tempted to discuss my own suspicions with her, but I didn't have anything concrete yet, and I wasn't quite ready to admit that I did my own investigating. Even to me, it sounded a bit ridiculous.

I replied, "You may be right. They say that intuition improves with age. So you should be super, super intuitive." I smiled and sipped my coffee.

"Oh, go piss up a rope."

I laughed out loud. "Seriously though, if I come across any mysteries that need solving, you can be my Watson."

She seemed placated, and we rushed through the rest of our breakfast in silence. Apparently, we were both anxious to get to work on the museum.

I used the switch at the top of the stairs to turn on the museum lights, then ran ahead to the Étienne exhibit to switch on the tape recorder. Mysterious music floated through the halls of the museum.

With a puzzled look, Dottie followed the source of the music to the new display. "Oh wow, you've been busy. Working late without me, I see!"

"I saved the fun part for you. We need to show Étienne being tortured and eaten by the Huron Indians. I was thinking we could have him screaming in agony as an Indian warrior removes his heart, and Indian women and children could be sitting near the fire, eating his cooked hands."

I was expecting her to be shocked, but I was disappointed. She just nodded while visualizing the scene. She said, "I already have the figures, but I'll need to get creative for the cooked hands and his face. I know we have some wax heads of soldiers who are shouting, so I could re-purpose one of them to make it look like Étienne is in pain. I could probably do the hands with paint, but we have equipment in the back room to make our own wax hands from scratch, if we need to."

"Good to know," I said. "Okay, let's start by getting rid of the junk."

We set aside an area of the floor to put items that could be sold or given away, and another for pure trash. There were old suitcases and bicycles everywhere, along with a hundred other things that looked like they came from a flea market.

"How did the tenants get their stuff down here?" I wondered out loud. "The museum and store should have been locked."

Dottie said, "There used to be a door that separated the store from the stairs to the apartments, but at some time after the store closed, somebody took it off its hinges."

I surveyed their junk and giveaway piles and shook my head in disbelief. "How are we going to get rid of all this stuff? The garbage truck already came by this morning."

Dottie waved her hand in the air dismissively. "Oh, that's easy. We put it on the street with a sign saying help yourself. A lot of merchandise changes hands that way in this city. You don't earn any money like you would with a garage sale, but in the long run everything balances out. You might find something on the street that you want yourself some day."

While I sorted through our growing junk piles, Dottie rummaged through a storage area under the stairs. Before long, she exclaimed, "I found the outdoor sign! I was afraid it was lost."

I helped her drag it out for a better look, and read the sign out loud: *Quebec In Wax. Gift Shop and Museum.*

Dottie studied the large sign and frowned.

"What's wrong?" I asked.

"I'm afraid we can't use this."

"Why not? It's perfect." And using it would save me a ton of money. I could finally check something off my list.

But Dottie burst my bubble. "There was a sign law passed in Quebec. It has to be in French."

I was disappointed. Dollar signs danced in front of my eyes. Signs, I knew, could be pricey. I scratched my head. "You know, this might be a blessing in disguise. Truth be told, the sign is a little boring. I have an idea for something a little more spectacular. We can make a new sign for a fraction of the cost."

I sketched out my idea for a sign and showed it to Dottie. "What do you think? Is it too showy?"

Any doubt I had disappeared. Dottie looked impressed. Mightily impressed. "Fantastic!"

"Then it's settled. I'll do it today," I said, adding it to the top of my mental list.

We returned to the area under the stairs to search for more treasures. "Hello, what have we here?"

There were several plastic storage boxes full of unopened merchandise from the old store. "Oh man, we've got loads of brand new things here!"

Dottie let out a cheer and helped me stack them at the bottom of the stairs to take up to the shop.

Tucked in behind these boxes at the very back of the storage area, I found a cardboard wardrobe box overflowing with cloth and fabric. Dottie recognized the large red shape that took up the bulk of the box, "Those are the velvet curtains that used to be at the bottom of the stairs! They add so much drama to the place."

I returned my attention to the box, which was now empty except for some curtain hardware, and a rolled-up rug. I cleared a spot on the floor and unrolled it for a closer look.

It was a heavy woven rug with sharp details, depicting what I assumed was a historical Quebec City scene. There were mountains in the background, and a ship unloading women onto the beach. On one side of the picture, white men were exchanging furs with the Indians. In another part of the scene, important-looking men shook hands with one another—judging by their clothes, they might have been the city founders. Overall, the picture was like something you'd find on the cover of a high school geography textbook. And I had certainly seen a lot of textbook covers in my time. Mostly because I'd never actually opened them.

The threads of the rug shimmered even under the dim museum lighting. It was a beautiful piece of work. We marveled at it while I decided how best to use it in the museum.

"I think it's too nice to use as a carpet," I said. "The foot traffic would destroy it. My grandmother had something like this hanging on her wall, except hers was a Northwest Territories scene of trappers shooting wolves."

We both stood back and stared at it.

Finally, with furrowed brows, I looked at Dottie. "Should we hang it in the shop?"

"I think we should hang it down here somewhere. It suits the museum because of the historical subject matter, and it gives people something extra to look at. We could type up a little information card and tack it underneath."

I nodded and gave her a thumbs up. "It seems like our *to do* list is getting longer, but nothing is being crossed off. Do you mind if I step out for a bit? I want to run some errands and buy supplies for our new sign."

"Okay, Paul. I'll get cracking on the Étienne exhibit; maybe I can get it all done this afternoon. By the way, tomorrow I won't be coming in, so you'll be on your own."

I was pleased by how things with Dottie were working out. I wasn't sure how I'd have managed without her. And it was nice just to have company. She seemed more like family every day.

I left her to her work and headed out.

My first order of business was to do some research on our new rug. I knew the perfect place to get answers on Quebec antiques.

But I had a bad feeling of what might happen if I went there.

Chapter 8

The rug was too awkward and heavy to lug around town, so I ran upstairs to fetch my high resolution camera. It was a gift from my mother, who'd made me promise to document my cross-country adventure with photos and regular emails. So far, I'd only taken pictures through the windshield of my van, so I was anxious to try an indoor shot.

I unrolled the rug in front of the large shop window. Even though natural light gives a fairly accurate color reproduction, I did a quick white-balance calibration using a sheet of paper. Then I cranked up the resolution and took my picture, making sure to fill the entire image frame and keep my hands steady while depressing the shutter. Pleased with the result, I headed to Tremblay's Antiques to see if I could persuade my arch enemy, Napoleon Roy, to take a look at it.

I doubted he'd give me a warm welcome, but I'd never win him over if I didn't try.

When I saw that Tremblay's still had police tape stretched across the door, I decided to try the library instead. I remembered seeing it on the way to Francine's costume shop, a modern glass and steel structure hiding in the back alleys behind the elegant historic buildings like an illegitimate child. It took a few minutes of searching before I finally found it again.

I circled the library to find the main entrance, then headed straight for the information desk.

The man at the counter had a waxed moustache and

slicked back hair. His long silk scarf was wrapped high around his neck as if he were a European playboy or had a throat infection. His weary eyes sized me up in an instant. "The youth hostel is down the street."

I smiled at him. I knew his type—flattery was the key. I just wondered how much sarcasm I could use without him picking up on it. "Wow! Is this the library or a Milan runway? That scarf is incredible."

His face lit up and he touched his scarf with his fingers. "This old thing? I've had it for days!" He smiled and straightened up. "Sorry for being a prickle puss. Now, how can I help you?"

"I'm not sure," I said. "I just bought a place nearby, and I found some cool things in a basement museum that I want to research. So antique books, I guess."

His face registered surprise. "Ah, the wax museum! You've created quite the little buzz around here, uh, Mister—"

"Paul," I said, "Paul Wainscott."

"My name is Gaillard, but in English it's Gaylord, so you can pronounce it that way if you prefer. Gaillard Duval."

"Nice to meet you. I like your accent. Are you from France?"

"Yes! The accent is much different here. It's actually hard for me to understand sometimes. I think I need a translator."

"You and me both," I admitted.

"Don't worry, your appalling French will improve if you work at it. But you mentioned antiques. I'm somewhat of an expert; my background is in history and antiquities, you know."

"Great! It sounds like you're the perfect person to help. For starters, I found an interesting rug that I want to learn more about."

"What sort of rug?"

I pulled out my camera and showed him the picture. "It was too large to bring with me."

His hands shook as he held the camera and squinted at the screen. "This is quite possibly the most exquisite tapestry I've ever seen!"

A few patrons looked up from their tables, so Gaillard Duval lowered his voice and led me to an old-fashioned card catalogue. He noticed my bewilderment as he pulled out a narrow file drawer. "We've just begun to computerize. Everything in this blasted library is stuck in time." He shook his head and mumbled while he flipped through the index cards. "Hey kids, why not create your resume on one of our manual typewriters, then you can use one of our fax machines to send it to the nineties..."

He slammed the drawer shut and I followed him to a tall shelf at the back of the library.

He offhandedly stacked books into my arms, clearly searching for something in particular. After a while, he put his hands on his narrow hips and looked puzzled. "We have several books on tapestries, but they've all been signed out. But the books you have here will be a good start. Your tapestry depicts a scene from the eighteenth century, so I included a book on that period."

We returned to the information desk. Gaillard typed my address and phone number into his computer and issued me a library card. Then he quickly glanced around the room, and leaned forward so that he wouldn't be overhead.

"If you want to learn everything there is to know about tapestries, visit Marie Tremblay at the Settlement Museum. She's the curator there and knows all about French antiquities. I work for her at the archaeological dig. You'll absolutely adore her; she's my dearest friend and mentor."

"Thanks for the tip," I said, wondering if Marie Tremblay was in any way related to the deceased Guy Tremblay.

When I reached for my new library card, Gaillard suddenly seized my wrist, "I *must* see that tapestry in person."

Gaillard certainly was dramatic. But I admired his passion for history—or at least, I hoped that was what his passion was for. I freed my arm from his clammy grasp and pocketed my card. "You're welcome to stop by some time if you like. I could use some advice on some exhibits I'm planning."

"You're re-opening the museum? How exciting!"

"I think so. I want to show the exciting and dark side of history, rather than the dry old history you get from text books."

Gaillard said, "You could show the cholera epidemic of 1832; thousands of people died from that." He paused, searching his mind for ideas. "Oh! You could show King Henri being stabbed in his coach in 1610. That's sensational and historically important."

"Both great ideas; I'll make sure to have a pad of paper and pen ready for your visit. You're a fountain of information."

"I should hope so, Paul. I have my Masters in French history and an undergraduate degree in archaeology. I like to think all that education is good for something—lord knows it doesn't pay well."

I shrugged, "Money isn't everything. I'm opening a wax museum. I don't expect to be rolling in dough either."

"Regrettably, I have expensive tastes," Gaillard said, passing me the bag of books. "I'd like to do something I love *and* get rich, too. Anyway, I'm pretty busy between the dig site and the library, but I'll try to stop by on the weekend."

On my way out the door, I glanced back toward the desk.

Gaillard was on the phone gesticulating wildly with his hand cupped over the receiver.

I introduced myself at the security desk of the Settlement Museum. The guard placed a call to Marie Tremblay's office, talked for a few moments, then hung up.

"She'll see you," he said. "Take the elevator on the left. You're going to room 224. But you'll need to sign this book and include your address and phone number."

It seemed excessive, but I jotted down my personal details anyway. As I crossed the expansive marble lined atrium to the elevators, I noticed at least a half a dozen security cameras. I'd wondered why the guard didn't ask to see my identification. I could have written anything down and he'd have been none the wiser. But now it was clear why. The cameras were tracking and recording my every move. There was even a camera in the corner of the waiting elevator.

I rode the elevator to the second floor and located Marie's office without any trouble; it was the only one in sight and had a plastic sign attached to it that read *Marie Tremblay*, with *Curator* beneath it in a smaller font.

I knocked lightly on her door. I could smell perfume and hear someone shuffling papers inside.

"Come on in," a voice said.

When I stepped into her office, I found that Marie Tremblay made a strong visual impression. She was a solid-looking woman with a big head of hair that was black and wiry like a chimney sweep's broom. She wore oversized jewelry that jangled noisily when she stood to greet me. Although I could tell she was making an effort to look composed and professional, her reddened eyes suggested either crying or drug use. I'd put money on the former.

Her office was architecturally cold and sterile like the rest of the modern museum, but she'd used every trick in the book to make it feel more warm and comfortable. Antique paintings hung haphazardly on the white walls, no doubt chosen for their covering ability rather than subject matter. Sitting on pedestals of varying heights all around the room, exotic-looking artifacts glowed under intense halogen lights.

On the credenza behind her desk, there was an old photo of her at an archaeological dig wearing shorts and a T-shirt. She was smiling and pretty then. The woman behind the desk was now precisely the opposite.

She followed my gaze. "That's me before I became a bureaucrat, a lifetime ago," she said, rising to shake my hand. "But don't let my appearance fool you. I can still swing a pick-axe, and in fact, I still work at the dig site when I have time."

I believed her about handling an axe. Her grip was firm, and her bare arms looked muscular. She struck me as a force of nature who could be pleasant one moment, and stormy and vicious the next.

"My name is Marie Tremblay."

"I'm Paul Wainscott. Thanks for seeing me. To be honest, I thought it would be a lot harder to see you. I'm sure it's a lot of work running a museum."

"Usually I don't meet with the public," she said. "We have a media liaison for that. And this is a particularly hectic week. But I received an intriguing call from Gaillard Duval. He said you had something to show me?" She gestured to a chair. "Please, have a seat."

I settled into one of the space-age leather chairs that faced her desk. It made a farting sound as I tried to make myself comfortable.

"I'll try to be brief," I said. "I just moved to the city, and I came across a rug while I was cleaning up my new place—well, I guess it's a tapestry—and I thought it would make a good exhibit. So I'm trying to learn more about it."

I switched on my camera and handed it to her.

Ms. Tremblay plugged it into her computer. In a few moments, her screen filled with a thumbnail gallery of my pictures. She searched through my images impatiently: blurry action shots of Beachley, some selfies I'd taken of myself in the bathroom, and a few pictures of tasty crêpes.

When she located the tapestry image, she expanded it to fill her screen.

Without taking her eyes from the screen, she rummaged through her giant purse and produced a pair of reading glasses, then leaned in for a closer look.

It was a full minute before she spoke.

Chapter 9

Marie Tremblay stood up and locked her door, then pressed some buttons on her phone.

"I'm setting it to voice mail," she said, attempting a smile. "Where did you say you found this tapestry? It should be in a museum."

"Really? I found it in my basement. I thought it was a cheap old rug, so I was going to put it on the floor of my gift shop."

"Horrifying," she said, shaking her head. "My specialty is baroque French artifacts, so I can tell you that this is not just an old rug." She gestured to her screen. "This was made by the famous Gobelins textile factory in Paris."

She had my full attention.

"The Gobelins factory started as a dye works in the 15th century. King Henry IV turned it into a tapestry factory in the seventeenth century and hired the best Flemish weavers. Later, King Louis XIV put a man named Jean Baptist Colbert in charge of the factory, intending to create the finest tapestries in the world. Yours is from that period. It probably took several years to make."

Her enthusiasm was contagious. I couldn't believe something like that was in my basement, and wondered what other treasures might be lurking there. "The image doesn't do it justice," I said, proud of my find. "It's even more amazing when sunlight hits it."

Marie nodded. "I'm not surprised. The shimmering colors are what make the Gobelins tapestries so famous.

Not only did they use over ten thousand colors of wool, they also used threads of gold, silver and silk. And this is why these tapestries are so rare. Many were burned during the French Revolution to extract the precious metals. I'm sure I haven't seen this particular tapestry before, because it depicts an important French Canadian scene."

"I was going to ask about that next," I said. "There's a whole lot going on in that picture."

She magnified the photo on her screen and scrolled across it. "I don't see a title, but given the way tapestries were named back then, I imagine it would have a title such as *The Establishment of Quebec City*. I would date it... late 17th century."

I helped myself to a notepad and pen from her desk, and began scribbling down the details. "Who do you think commissioned this one?"

"Tapestries from the Baroque period often depict historical events. Nobility loved to have representations of their lives that they could hang on their wall to impress their friends. It was the ultimate status symbol, and very few people could afford them. Considering their price and the amount of time it took to make one, they were usually gifts from kings. I'm only guessing at this point, but this tapestry would have been commissioned by someone very important, maybe even King Louis XIV himself."

"Wow." I sat back in my chair and took a deep breath, tapping my pen on the notepad. "So, do you think Frontenac brought it over from France?"

"No, the timing doesn't fit. We do know Jean Talon travelled between Quebec and France around that time, so it's possible that he brought it back with him. Perhaps it was given to Frontenac to commemorate his second term as Governor."

I looked at the tapestry on her screen, lost in the

wonder of it. "So what is the scene we're looking at?"

She moved around the image with her mouse. "Well, obviously that's the Saint Lawrence river in the background, and the King's daughters are getting off the ship. Since there was a shortage of women in Quebec, the king sent women over to bolster the population. The man welcoming them off the boat could be Jean Talon, and the crowd of people are the settlers." Marie zoomed in on a group of Indians holding furs and guns. "This would represent Champlain's trading outpost where natives could exchange items for French goods. Trade was a big part of the city."

She moved her mouse pointer over a man wearing silver-buckled shoes, with a fashionable cloak, sword, lace cuffs, and a feather in his hat. "The most incredible part of the tapestry is these men in the foreground. The man on the left would be Frontenac, and next to him is Champlain."

"Why is that incredible?" I asked.

"Because there are no known images of Samuel Champlain in existence. Since this tapestry was made close to the time when he lived, we could very well be looking at his true image."

My excitement was at an all time high now. Maybe I could sell the tapestry? I hated to ask Marie something so crass, but I couldn't help myself. "What do you think it would be worth?"

"As I said, there are only a few Gobelins left, owned by Parisian dealers. But for Canada, it has even more significance, and it appears to be in perfect condition." She paused for a moment. "At auction, it could sell for a million dollars, possibly more. I'd love to see it in person."

I smiled. "I'll bring it over some day, if you like. Assuming I can find an armored car on short notice."

"That sounds wonderful," she said, standing up. "If you're really interested in this stuff, I can give you a tour of the dig site. I'm supervising it tomorrow. Just come by around ten in the morning."

I smiled and stood up to leave. "I look forward to it; thanks!"

My mind was racing as I left Marie's office, and I almost collided with Bernard in the hallway. He looked surprised to see me. "Paul! What brings you here?"

"I was going to ask you the same thing," I said, looking him over, "but I guess it's pretty obvious."

"Oh, you mean my uniform," Bernard said, "Yeah I'm a security guard here. Not very glamorous, but it pays the bills in between clients." When he saw my confusion, he lowered his voice and said, "Keep this under wraps—I just got my agent license and started my own private investigating firm. No clients yet, but here's hoping." He crossed his fingers.

"Good for you! Speaking of investigations, have you heard anything about Guy's murder?"

"Unfortunately I'm not in the loop, and Landry is being tight-lipped about it. I'm tempted to tackle the case myself. Maybe I could make a name for myself as a private investigator."

"Good idea. Why don't you stop by for a coffee sometime? I have a full schedule today, but maybe around lunch time tomorrow?"

"Sure, I might do that. I can always find time for coffee. It's a habit from my years on the police force; I still crave coffee and baked goods," he said with a laugh.

I wrote my phone number on a slip of paper and handed it to Bernard. He tipped his hat and rushed off to answer a call on his walkie-talkie.

Chapter 10

A million dollars!

On the walk home I couldn't stop thinking about all that money. I could pay off the mortgage on my building and be set for life. Regrettably, the tapestry probably wasn't mine to sell. But it was still fun to dream.

I crossed a gravel parking lot and came across the Pétanque game that Guy had mentioned.

The players looked like overgrown babies playing marbles. They were bald, overweight, and heavily tanned. Each of them wore small shorts and a thick gold necklace. The day was a scorcher, but the men seemed content as lizards under a heat lamp.

I was relieved to see that Napoleon wasn't among them, although having him there could have given me an opportunity to get to know him better. The last thing I wanted was an enemy when starting my new life. And frankly, I had no idea what Napoleon had against me.

One person I did recognize was Detective Landry. It was a bit unsettling to see him out of his police uniform.

Next to him stood a man who looked like a French longshoreman, with a sagging leathery face, a five o'clock shadow, and a cigarette drooping from his mouth.

The third man was the youngest. He hadn't yet taken on the pear-shaped body and dark skin of his compatriots, but it wouldn't be long until his transformation was complete. He appeared to be of

Spanish descent, with hair just starting to turn grey at the temples. He was the first one to notice my presence, and approached me with a warm smile.

"Hello, my friend! I'm Pascal Gigot. We could use a fourth player, if you want to play."

Before I could answer, Landry spotted me and walked over to join us.

"This is Paul Wainscott," Landry said. "He just moved to the city and bought the old wax museum." He turned to me. "You're welcome to play, Napoleon won't show today, so we could use a fourth."

"I guess Napoleon has a lot on his mind," I said.

"He's under a lot of stress; he took Guy's death hard."

The Frenchman with the drooping cigarette walked over on bandied legs, laughing from one side of his mouth with his cigarette securely wedged in the other. "If Napoleon shows up, he can team up with Paul and share their balls. I know he'd like that."

He burst into laughter, but it dissolved into coughing. He composed himself and shook my hand. "My name is Francois LeCompte."

"Nice to meet you," I said. "I've never played this game. I'd hate to spoil it for you guys."

Francois said, "Nonsense! We all have to learn some time. You can be on my team. I'll teach you everything I know."

"I think you already did," Detective Landry joked.

Francois walked over to an ice cooler and fished out a can. "First things first," he said, tossing me a beer, "This will help your aim. Last thing you want to do is think too much."

"I like this game already," I said with a smile. "I'm a fan of any sport that involves standing around and drinking. Should I take my shirt off too?"

Pascal pretended to be serious as he looked me up

and down. "No way. I kind of like being the best looking one in our group."

Francois looked hurt and patted his fat stomach. "I thought I was the one with the looks?"

"Yah," Landry complained, "I thought it was me."

They all laughed.

"Okay, let's get serious," Francois said. "This game is named Pétanque, which loosely means "feet anchored," because you have to make all your throws from the same spot." He motioned to a 2-foot circle that was scratched into the hard dirt. "We take turns throwing, trying to get as close as possible to the jack. That's the smaller ball over there. You earn one point for every ball that's closer to the jack than anyone else's."

"That's it?" I asked.

"Pretty much," he replied.

"And this game is a big deal around here?"

"Hell yes! There are even world championships."

I picked up one of the hollow metal balls that lay near my feet and weighed it in my hand. "I'm ready; let's do this."

Francois gathered up the red balls and kicked the blue ones over to Pascal and Landry using his bare feet. "You guys start. I'm going to strategize with my new partner here."

Landry went over and made a show of dragging the beer cooler as far as possible from where we stood. "I know what your idea of strategizing is, Pascal. Leave some *strategy* for the rest of us."

They all laughed.

Francois stood in the circle and tossed the small jack into the air. It landed with a thud about twenty feet away, sending up a tiny cloud of dust.

Landry replaced him in the circle, and prepared to throw one of his balls. He crouched down with his arm held straight out in front of him, frozen in position, waiting for just the right moment. When that moment came, he popped up to make his throw.

Just before he released the ball, Francois shouted, "You stink!"

The ball traced a steep arc and landed several feet short of its target and rolled off to one side. Landry glared at Francois as he switched places with him in the circle.

As Francois got ready to throw his ball, he glanced back and forth between Landry and the little jack in the sand. He threw the ball, and it came to rest just short of Landry's ball, even further away from the jack.

Pascal laughed. "We can move the jack if you guys want?"

Francois turned to me. "You're up, kid. We have to keep going until one of us gets closer."

I took my spot in the circle and held the ball in the air, trying to gauge how much force I should use. I'd been a starting pitcher in high school, so I was fairly accurate at long distances. But this was different. For starters, it required an underhand throw. Instead of throwing straight and hard at my target, I had to let gravity do a lot of the work.

"Look at the intensity in his face!" Francois said with a chuckle.

Ignoring him, I leaned forward and threw the ball in a gentle curve toward the jack. The direction was perfect, but everything else I did was off, so the ball landed a couple of feet directly behind the jack. It appeared to be same distance from the jack as Landry's ball.

Landry whistled. "Nice throw there, Paul."

"We're gonna need a surveyor to check this one," Pascal joked. He unclipped a measuring tape from his belt and measured the distance of the closest balls to the jack.

"What's the verdict, inspector? Measuring tape not long enough?" Landry asked.

"Looks like Paul is still further," Pascal concluded. "You're up, Francois."

Francois' ball also landed long, so it was time for me to take my next shot.

"The jack is dying of loneliness," Landry joked, "He wants some company." They all laughed.

My second ball landed very close to the jack, but I made the angle too low and it rolled past all the other balls.

"You've got to put backspin on it, so it lands flat," Francois said. He demonstrated the correct motion on his next throw. The ball sailed through the air and came to rest right next to the jack, nudging it.

"Hey, Michael," Pascal said to Landry, stifling a burp. "Don't they automatically lose if they hit the jack?"

Chuckling, the other team threw the rest of their balls, trying to get one closer to the jack than Francois had. Their final ball was a direct hit on the Frenchman's, sending it completely out of the playing area. The other team was in a position to win by four balls, and we only had two more chances to do something about it: Francois' last throw, and then mine.

"Alright, bro, sneak in there," I said.

His ball landed within an inch of the jack. While not good enough to win, it would at least limit the other team to winning a single point.

Francois shook his head while he lit a fresh cigarette. "It's all up to you now, Paul. You gotta look sharp; there could be a scout for the world championships here!" Then he laughed and started to cough again.

All eyes were on me now. I could still win the game. "I can throw it any way I like, right?"

"You can throw it like Twinkle Toes Flintstone for all we care," Landry said. He paused to guzzle some beer, then wiped his mouth with the back of his hand.

I stood tall and turned my body at a right angle to the jack. I wound up like a baseball pitcher, and threw it overhand in a way I'd done thousands of times before, keeping my fingers on top of the ball and my elbow at shoulder height. I used just enough speed to deliver it accurately to the jack. It smashed into the dirt right in front of the blue balls that were shielding it, causing a chain reaction that resulted in the jack rolling backward two feet—directly into our waiting balls.

Pascal and Landry threw up their hands and groaned. The Frenchman's face lit up in joy. "Wow! What form! You should be in the major leagues, Paul!"

"Time for more strategizing," Pascal said.

I could tell everyone was a little inebriated, so I realized this might be a perfect chance to get some information. We all made our way to the picnic table and beer cooler.

"You're welcome to play with us any time," Pascal said to me. "If you don't mind hanging out with a bunch of *senile* citizens that is."

"What are you talking about," I said, "you're not old."

"I was referring to these guys," he said with a laugh, gesturing at the others.

"It sounds fun, but I wouldn't want to be a fifth wheel."

"Because of Napoleon, you mean? He doesn't seem to like you much, does he? Well, he'll come around. He wasn't my biggest fan when we first met either."

"That's good to know," I said, then quickly added, "That didn't come out right. I meant it's good to know he might come around, not that he didn't like you. How long have you lived here?"

Pascal smiled. "I moved here a few years ago from Argentina with my wife and daughter. I studied at the university here to become a civil engineer. I joined this Pétanque game last year. Napoleon didn't like me because I couldn't speak French very well."

Landry held up a finger to interrupt. "It goes much beyond French with you though, Paul. Napoleon is a separatist, and it's true that he does have a prejudice against English speakers living in Quebec. But with you, the problem also involves your building."

"He doesn't want an Anglophone buying a historic French building?" I asked.

"No, he doesn't want *you* buying *his* building."

I was confused. "His building?"

Landry waved dismissively with his free hand, "He's being ridiculous, of course. But you have to understand that he has a strong sentimental connection to it. He lived there with his own family many years ago, and then as a caretaker for many years since. He undertook countless renovations and repairs without being paid a cent for his work. All because he was under the impression that Guy would sell him the building one day. Of course, Guy made no effort to set him straight, because he was getting free labor."

I winced. "That's awful. I can see where the animosity is coming from."

I tried to keep an open mind about people. Heck, all surfers wipe out from time to time, both the good ones and the bad ones. The ocean doesn't discriminate, so I shouldn't either.

"There's also Guy's murder," Landry added. "They'd known each other for a long time, so his death has to have hit him hard."

This was my chance. As casually as possible, I asked, "How's the investigation coming along?"

"You know I can't discuss the case with you."

"Why not? Guy was a good friend of my family. I came here because of him."

Landry seemed to mull it over. "Maybe I'll make a little exception here, since you might be able to help me. What do you know about your boarder?"

"You mean Remy? Not a lot. Why?"

"I've been trying to locate him. Have you seen him?"

"Now that you mention it, I haven't seen him today. But I haven't been here long enough to know if that's unusual. What's this all about?"

Landry sighed. "I may as well tell you. And don't repeat this to anyone. Guy had a security camera in the front room of his store pointed toward the sales counter. In the footage from the night before Guy's murder, someone can be seen watching Guy through the window with his nose pressed against the glass."

"He has a lot of cool stuff in that store," I said. "So what's strange about that?"

He paused. "You're right; there's a lot of interesting things in that store, so it has more than its fair share of looky-loos. But this individual had his face painted completely white. Like a mime."

I headed home from the Pétanque game with a lot to think about.

I thought about what Guy had said about *Pure Laine* when I'd spoken to him on my first day. In essence, the tapestry was like a physical embodiment of *pure wool*—a connection to the past, physically and symbolically. A weaving of threads and precious metals, like the many old connections formed between people of the city and their past. It was far too valuable, historically and financially, to be left unprotected.

I quickened my pace, cursing myself for wasting so

much time playing Pétanque. I reminded myself that this was one of the safest cities in North America, so I should have nothing to worry about. The odds of being broken into today should be astronomically low.

When I neared my building, I was surprised to find Beachley relaxing on the sidewalk. She ran to me with her tail wagging.

I scratched her head. "What're you doing out here, buddy? Did Remy let you out?"

She just tilted her head and panted. I wondered how long she'd been outside in the sun without water, and was upset that somebody had let her get out.

But my anger turned to alarm when I saw that my door was open, with splinters of wood around the latch.

My heart sank as I entered the shop.

The boxes I'd brought upstairs were overturned, their contents were strewn everywhere. I rushed into the kitchen, where I had foolishly left the tapestry on the kitchen table. I may as well have put a *take me* note on it.

My worst nightmare had come true. The tapestry was gone.

Some lame ass had taken it.

Chapter 11

My usual tendency in a crisis was to flip out. I had a lot of respect for people who could always remain calm, and I wanted to be more like them.

In actual fact, it wasn't the end of the world. I was no worse off than I was before I'd found the tapestry. Messes could be cleaned up, broken locks could be fixed. As for the overturned boxes of merchandise, well, they didn't contain anything too valuable anyway.

I wondered who could have taken the tapestry. Who even knew it existed?

To start with, there was Gaillard Duval at the library. He'd showed a keen interest in the rug, and he knew right where to find it.

Then there was Marie Tremblay. Not only had she been blown away when she saw it, she understood its full value. She could have read my address from the sign-in book at the security desk. If she took it, that might explain why she'd made no attempt to acquire the tapestry for the Settlement museum when I had been there. As a curator, that should have been her first instinct. Maybe it was because she was planning to acquire it for herself, instead?

But ultimately, my instincts pointed to Napoleon. As an antiques dealer, he would also appreciate the value of the tapestry, and he seemed capable of almost anything. He might have broken in out of pure mischief, and come across the tapestry by accident. Granted, he wouldn't have needed to break the locks to gain entry since he almost certainly had kept a copy of my key for himself when he'd changed the locks. Unless, of course, he realized that using his key would point directly to him.

That left Dottie, a possibility that was almost too ridiculous to consider. She could have known more about the tapestry than she let on. How could she not have recognized it, when she knew every square inch of the museum? You could buy a pretty sweet world cruise with that much money. And why did Beachley bark when she first arrived? Had she been touching my things?

I took out Detective Landry's card and gave him a call. He should still be at the Pétanque game.

It only rang once. "Landry here."

"Hi, this is Paul Wainscott."

The detective perked up. "Everything alright?"

"I'm afraid not. My building was broken into."

"I'm in homicide. That has nothing to do with me," he said gruffly. Then he sighed. "But since I'm close by, I'll stop over. Don't go anywhere. I'll be around in an hour or so."

I heard a click and the line went dead.

An hour or so? He's actually going to finish his Pétanque game?

I fed Beachley and put a kettle of water on to boil. Suddenly, I remembered the apartments upstairs.

I rushed up the stairs two at a time. Who knows what else the thief might have taken, or if he was still in the building!

Sure enough, all of the rooms had been broken into. The thief must have started by ransacking the guest rooms. If he'd searched the main level first, he would have found the tapestry in the kitchen and left immediately.

Fortunately, my own room only contained my unpacked bags and an alarm clock—just what I could fit into the van for my cross-country odyssey without crowding Beachley. The rest of my possessions were being shipped from Vancouver. So there was nothing of any real value, and nothing appeared to be missing.

Remy's room wasn't so lucky. Every drawer had been yanked out and dumped on the floor. He had a small wooden computer desk with an laptop sitting on it. Several books had fallen on the floor next to the desk, including some large books on tapestries. I could tell by the Dewey decimal numbers on their spines that they came from the library.

I hit the spacebar on his laptop to wake it from hibernation. His browser was open to a car dealership specializing in exotic cars—Remy appeared to be building his dream car online. It wasn't unusual for a young guy to dream about cars he couldn't afford, but Francine had mentioned that Remy believed he was coming into a lot of money.

The kettle started to whistle downstairs, so I returned to the kitchen to make myself a coffee.

With so many problems over the past few days, I was surprised by how calm I was. Maybe a change of scenery was exactly what I needed.

It was as good a time as any to sample the dark truffles I had bought. Even though I was on a strict high protein, low carb diet, I rationalized that all the excitement of the past few days would burn a lot of calories. Not to mention, I needed to fuel my brain to maximize my thinking power. I sat down at the table and started to pop truffles into my mouth.

Remy thought that he was coming into money, and he was researching tapestries. Right here, in my building, there was an extremely valuable tapestry. So it was probably safe to conclude that the tapestry belonged to Remy, and he was hiding it in the basement.

But where did he get it from? Did he find it in the basement too, or was it stolen? And if it was stolen, from whom?

My thoughts returned to Guy. Could the tapestry be involved in Guy's murder? Did Remy get caught while stealing the tapestry from Tremblay Antiques, and then kill Guy after a struggle? The soft-spoken mime didn't seem capable of murder, but wasn't it always the person you least suspected?

I decided to tidy up while waiting for Detective Landry to arrive. There were only a few days remaining before I had to open my doors for business, and I was running out of time.

Beachley followed me from her rug near the fireplace into the gift shop. "Have you come to help?"

She just wagged her tail. She'd been sticking close to me since we arrived, probably feeling insecure in our new place, and also from being left outside after the break-in. I wondered if Beachley had given the thief any trouble, or if she just watched indifferently with her tail wagging as he ransacked the rooms.

I dragged the boxes of basement merchandise into the middle of the room and started unpacking. I was pleased to see that most of the items already had price tags. They were reasonably priced for the era when the museum had closed down, but considering that several decades had passed, they were practically a steal now. But regardless of what price I put on the items, the mark-up on these items would 100% since I didn't actually buy the inventory myself. So I elected to leave the prices exactly as they were. Maybe it would help generate a lot of sales for my grand opening.

An hour later, all of the sticks, pens, shirts, snow-globes, and other souvenirs were neatly displayed on the shelves. My inventory was still sparse, but at least the store looked respectable now. Besides, I was always of the opinion that having too much inventory just made everything look cheaper as a whole.

A loud knock snapped me out of my thoughts.

I figured it must be Detective Landry, but I was wrong.

The outline of a huge man loomed outside my front door, a dark shadow framed by the bright sun behind him.

Chapter 12

The knocking came with a whiny voice. "I'm dying out here. Open the door!"

I found a very heavy and very sweaty man on my stoop, with dark wisps of hair combed across his bald scalp. He might have weighed over four hundred pounds, but without an industrial-sized scale one could only guess. If I were really curious, I could have taken him for a ride in my van and driven through one of those weighing stations, subtracting the weight with and without him inside. That's how they did it back home when a dead whale washed up on the beach.

The whale/man looked friendly and wore a cardigan sweater and pinstripe pants. He handed me a large water-speckled cardboard box and rubbed his arms to bring back the circulation, breathing heavily. "This came for you today. You weren't in, so they asked me to sign for it. There's another box in my store, even bigger than this one."

I checked the shipping label on the box. It was my new point of sale system. "Wow! I ordered this yesterday and didn't expect it this quickly. I'm Paul Wainscott, by the way."

The fat man was still wheezing when he shook my hand. "I'm Toby Farber. I own the bookstore next door. I've been meaning to come over and introduce myself, but I wanted to give you a chance to get settled in. What happened to your door?"

"Break-in," I said.

Toby's sweaty face registered surprise. "A break-in?

That's unheard of around here. We have the lowest crime rate in North America, you know. Did they get anything?"

"There wasn't anything to get, really." It was a lie, but I didn't see any reason to tell him about the tapestry. "Would you like a coffee? I make a pretty decent brew, if I say so myself."

"Splendid! I have a new employee working cash right now. This is good opportunity to see how she handles things if I leave her alone. So by all means, lead on!"

The coffee in the carafe was still hot. I wasn't going to tell him I'd just eaten or he might feel like he was putting me out; having more coffee and snacks was really the only polite course of action.

"Would you care for a pastry?" I asked.

Toby flopped heavily into a chair and brushed his few hairs into place with his fingers. "To be honest, Paul, I smelled them when I came in. At this point, if you didn't offer me one, I'd chew your arm off for a bite."

I laughed and put a caramel pastry puff on his plate. Toby narrowed his eyes and made a keep-them-coming gesture with his hand. I added a soft caramel cupcake on each of our plates and smiled. "I see I'm not the only one who likes these."

Toby nibbled one of the pastries like he was sampling a fine wine, then dug in with the urgency of a crack fiend. Moments later, he was brushing the crumbs from his hands. "These are from L'Ancienne Boulangerie. The best pastry puffs in the city. You've done well."

I sampled my own. The pastry puff had a sweet cheese curd filling and was packed with flavor.

Toby took a closer look at me. "You better be careful, I was in great shape like you once. Behold,

106 Death of a Dummy

your future!" He spread his arms with a dramatic flourish, and his shirt hiked up to reveal an enormous white beach ball. I felt a pang of dread.

Toby noticed my reaction and laughed heartily. Then he noticed there was still a cupcake on his plate and stuffed it in his mouth. He ate this one more slowly, as if hoping to prolong it.

"So how long have you had the bookstore?" I asked.

"Two years. I came here for a long vacation with my wife, not speaking a word of French. We loved the city so much that we decided to stay. Shortly after that, we learned the bookstore was for sale, and we snatched it up. My wife was a librarian in Toronto, and I love to read, so it was a good fit."

I laughed. "I thought you were born here. Why are we speaking French when we're both English?"

"It's a law, I think," Toby said, smiling.

I poured our coffees as Toby looked on expectantly. Then suddenly, he looked sad.

"I'm afraid I've eaten my snack too quickly, now I have a delicious coffee and nothing to enjoy with it," he said dejectedly.

"One step ahead of you, my friend," I said, and placed a whoopee pie on his plate.

"Ah," he said with a satisfying sigh. "I think we are going to be great friends." He took a sip of his coffee, clearly enjoying Dottie's special blend. "So, I notice you got yourself a LaserPOS point of sale system? Those are excellent; I was thinking of getting one myself. But I'm afraid it would take me forever to plug in all my inventory. I noticed your store is coming along well?"

I shrugged, "It will have to do for now. It's mostly stuff I picked up from other merchants to sell on consignment. Plus, I found some old merchandise in the basement."

Then I had an idea.

"You don't by any chance have some books that I could sell for you in my store? I wouldn't be able to place a large enough order myself to get reseller pricing, and I wouldn't want to directly compete with you anyway. We might as well work together, if you're willing."

"Good idea," Toby said. "Actually, I tried to buy this building from Guy a few times in the past. I need space to expand my store. So maybe this will help in a small way. What sort of books do you want?"

"Anything that would fit the theme of a wax museum. The dark history of Quebec or of Canada, that sort of thing."

"No problem, I have the perfect books in mind. I'll bring them over for you."

We were interrupted by man's voice from the next room, "Hello?"

"I'll go get those books for you, and the other box the courier dropped off. I'll be right back." With visible effort, Toby pulled himself up from the table and walked toward the front door, swaying heavily. He gave a perfunctory nod to my visitor on the way out.

Standing in the doorway, Detective Landry locked eyes with mine and flipped his notebook open like there was a list of places he'd rather be. "You, my friend, are bad luck."

"What do you mean?" I asked.

"You're here for a couple of days, and already we have a murder and a break-in. It's unprecedented, you know. Quebec City has the lowest crime rate in North America."

I rolled my eyes. "So I've heard. But I fail to see how any of this is my fault."

The detective just grunted and got right to business. "Anything missing?"

Suddenly, I wondered how much I should disclose to the police. Wasn't Detective Michael Landry a friend of Napoleon's? Who knows what types of connections run between these people. I didn't know who to trust anymore. I decided not to mention anything about the tapestry, at least until I had more information and could eliminate Napoleon Roy from my list of suspects.

"Not that I can tell," I replied. "But you'll have to ask Remy, my tenant."

"Any signs of forced entry?"

"Yeah, the door you just walked through."

He nodded and flipped his book shut. "I've got what I need. If there was nothing taken then there isn't much to follow up on. Just punks who saw an opportunity and took it. I checked with your neighbors and they didn't see anything, so there's not much more I can do. We'll be in touch."

"That's it?" I asked, dumbfounded. Maybe I'd made a mistake by not mentioning the tapestry. Without a big crime there was little motivation for the police to investigate.

"That's it." the detective replied. Then he left as quickly as he came.

I shook my head and turned my attention to my new point of sale system, unwrapping it like a child on Christmas morning. This system really had it all. It was a combination cash-register and sleek computer system that tracked your sales and inventory, generated reports, and even told you when to re-order based on sales forecasts. It was an expensive indulgence that I hoped would pay for itself many times over. And it was just plain cool.

I had it up and running quickly, and was starting to enter my meagre inventory into the system when Toby Farber returned, pushing several boxes of books on a mover's dolly.

"I left the big package by the door while you were talking to the detective. It looks like you bought yourself a great printer! Anyway, these are the books. Your shelves looked pretty empty so I figured I'd bring you a wide selection. You can return what you don't want to display."

"How much do I owe you for them?" I asked, looking around for my checks.

Toby shooed the idea away with his hand, "We'll do it on consignment. After you sell them, you can buy them from me for eighty percent of their cover price. That gives each of us a twenty percent mark-up."

"That sounds more than fair." I smiled and put a hand on his shoulder. "I really appreciate this, Toby. It almost looks like a store now."

"No sweat," Toby said.

Interesting choice of words, I thought.

Toby continued, "So you were saying something about re-opening the wax museum?"

"That's right. The shop will open first though; I still have a lot of work to do downstairs."

"I can imagine. I'd offer to help, but I've got my hands full training my new sales girl."

"I appreciate the thought. But I've got Dottie to help me out anyway."

Toby nodded. "She's a dynamo, that one. You're in good hands. Well, I better get back to my store. Stop by some time for coffee and I'll return the favor. I have some delicious treats that will knock your socks off." He glanced at my bare feet. "Well, you know what I mean."

"I'll take you up on that."

After Toby left, I looked at the time on my phone, and noticed several text messages from Francine. I must have been too distracted to feel the vibrations in my pocket. According to her texts, she was concerned that she hadn't heard from Remy all day. I responded that I'd let her know when he showed up.

Where could he be?

Chapter 13

Standing in my store window, I watched the tourists pass by, laughing and sharing animated conversations. The sun was just beginning to disappear behind the roofs of the buildings across the street.

For the first time since I'd arrived, I felt the urge to exercise. Although I'd meant to take a break from my strict fitness regiment, I didn't want to completely abandon it either. Besides, running helped me to relax and think, and I definitely had things to sort out.

I put on my running clothes and stepped out into the fresh night air, shutting the door firmly behind me. The lock was broken, but I figured the odds of being robbed twice in one day were profoundly low—especially since this city had the lowest crime rate in North America.

I started my run down a popular tourist street where a throng of slow-moving gastropods were on the prowl for food. Unfortunately for me, they stopped and changed directions whenever they passed an outdoor menu, which was nearly every building they passed. I had to duck and dodge between them, and even had a few near collisions, before I decided to take a detour to the stone battlements.

I ran along the grassy slopes and the stone wall surrounding the old city, enjoying how the air felt in my lungs as I worked up to my target pace. The city was beautiful when viewed from above: a fairytale panorama of copper roofs and cozy stone buildings, their warm lights twinkling in the growing darkness.

I ran up a flight of stone stairs to the highest point of the ancient wall, and stopped when I recognized a girl taking pictures with her small tripod resting on the wall.

"Sophie!" I shouted, as I came up behind her.

Sophie startled and spun around, knocking over her tripod with her hand. I reached out and stabilized it before it could tumble over the edge.

"Oopsy Daisy!" I said.

Oopsy daisy? Someone should toss *me* over the wall.

"Hi, Paul," she said. She gave me a grin that lit up her face. The sunset gave her skin a warm golden tone.

"Snagging a few shots?" I asked.

"Yup."

"I bet I look pretty awesome in this light," I said, swinging my long hair back and striking a pose. "Feel free to take a picture if you want some more fine art for your wall."

"Get over yourself," she laughed.

I looked out at the scene she was photographing. "Wow, killer sunset!"

"I know. It's beautiful, isn't it?" she said, following my gaze.

The cityscape outside the old walls spread out before us like an enormous model train set, framed on the horizon by the Laurentian mountains. The sky was streaked with clouds made deep crimson by the setting sun. What made the scene magic was the billowing smoke that filled the sky from stacks below. Seagulls from the Saint Laurence soared through the enormous exhaust clouds that seemed to glow as if lit from within.

"It's incredible," I said, "It would make a great postcard, but at the same time, it's artistic. It's kind of sad really, seeing those birds fly through the pollution. A juxtaposition of beauty and ugliness," I paused and looked into her eyes, "like the two of us."

She giggled and rolled her eyes at me. "You're not

ugly."

I feigned surprise. "Why do you automatically assume you're the beauty?"

We laughed and she punched my arm.

"Ouch. That's going to leave a mark," I said.

"Now you won't be so beautiful anymore," she replied, her eyes sparkling.

We smiled at each other for a few moments, then I broke the silence.

"So, do you come here often? I hate to think of you all by yourself with nobody to keep you company."

"I don't mind. I've been coming every night. Photography is like fishing; you have to wait for everything to be perfect: the lighting, the sky, and, in this case, the seagulls. And there are only a few good hours of the day for pictures. A lot of people think full sun is best for pictures, but actually it's the opposite."

"Really? Why is that?"

"Well, the colors are all washed out, there are hard shadows on everything, and the sky is too bright, so it usually comes out as solid white in your pictures. I'll take a cloudy day over a sunny day, any time."

I nodded, taking in the information. "So is that a telephoto lens?"

She bent down and peered into the viewfinder, adjusting the camera position. "Yup. I'm focusing on the big smoke stacks. Take a look."

I leaned in and looked through the camera. Sophie's face was very close to my own.

"Nice, we should start a camera club. Just you and me."

She smiled.

"Oh, I almost forgot," I said. "I have a proposition for you."

She looked suspicious. "A proposition?"

"Business related. I need some artwork for my guest

rooms, and thought maybe we could help each other out."

"What did you have in mind?"

"I thought maybe you could pick out a dozen or so of your best artsy-fartsy black and white photos, and I'll frame and hang them in my guest rooms with a price tag. When someone buys one, I subtract the money I spent on materials, and you get whatever is left. It won't cost you a thing, and you can put any price on them you like."

Sophie smiled and her eyes opened wide with excitement. "Wow, Paul, that's a great idea! I'd love to do that."

"We could also mount some of your color photos, and sell them unframed in the gift shop as pictures that they can't buy anywhere else. I'd take care of the printing and mats, and subtract that cost when someone buys."

"This is exciting!" she said. "I want to go home right now and start choosing images. I guess we're going to be working pretty closely on this, huh?"

"It never crossed my mind," I said with a grin, "but that's definitely a bonus."

I sighed and straightened up. "Well, I should let you get back to work."

"And you should get back to your running before you cool down," she added.

"No chance of that," I said with a wink, and started to jog away.

I continued my run along the wall of the old city until Quebec's landmark hotel, Chateau Frontenac, came into view. The sky was dark now, and the castle-like structure was illuminated by powerful spotlights. Next to the hotel and overlooking the river, a long wooden boardwalk was suspended above a rocky cliff. The boardwalk was illuminated by antique streetlights, and beneath one of them, a fire rescue truck and an ambulance looked jarringly out of place. A large crowd of people had gathered near the iron safety railing.

As I got closer, I could make out police uniforms in the crowd, and recognized the imposing figure of Detective Landry. I slowed to a walk and mixed in with the crowd at the railing.

Most of the gawkers appeared to be tourists, but there were also waiters and uniformed hotel employees who came outside to satisfy their curiosity. Everybody was looking over the railing, snapping pictures on their phones and pointing.

I braced myself for what I might see, and took a look.

Emergency floodlights were trained on something lying on a rocky shelf some twenty or thirty feet below. It appeared to be a bronze statue, with officers and paramedics crouching over it. My first thought was that vandals had tossed a statue from one of the city's fountains over the edge. But then I noticed white skin showing where a sleeve of the sculpture had been pulled back. It was covered in tattoos.

All at once, I realized it was Remy.

I stared at the scene below, unable to believe what I was seeing. I heard people nearby comparing notes. One said he'd heard that the victim was already dead when he went over the edge, having been stabbed in the chest. Another bystander added that the victim might not have fallen at all, since he knew for a fact that there was a narrow dirt path leading down to the platform.

Landry's commanding voice cut through the clamor. "Move along, folks. There's nothing to see here!"

"Sure there is," someone in the crowd hollered. "There's a guy down there with a pick-axe in his chest!"

The police were quickly dispersing the crowd, and I decided that I didn't want to be seen by Detective Landry at the scene of Unlikely Murder #2 in the city with a low crime rate. I took a final peek and then started home, with my mind racing.

I thought about Francine Chapelle. Her closest friend was now dead, most likely murdered. Correction. He was definitely murdered—unless he went over the railing carrying the pick-axe, and it came down on top of him after he landed. But things like that only happened to Wile E Coyote.

Who would want to kill Remy? Did this prove there was a connection to the tapestry and Guy's murder? One thing was for sure, my previous theory now seemed unlikely: that Remy had killed Guy after being caught stealing the tapestry. That would mean there were actually two killers on the loose.

In all likelihood, the same person who'd murdered Guy had murdered Remy. Perhaps the murderer thought Guy had the tapestry in his store, and the botched robbery had led to Guy's death. Then he'd realized that Remy had it, and killed him too.

I had lots of pieces, but they didn't quite fit together. Only a few things were certain: my old family friend was dead, my tenant was dead, and a priceless tapestry was missing.

I thought about my next appointment with Marie Tremblay in the morning. I needed to find out everything I could about the black market for antiquities.

Maybe if I found the tapestry, I'd also find the killer.

Chapter 14

I woke shortly before my appointment at the Settlement Museum. This suited me fine. I couldn't enjoy a breakfast while I was worried about Francine, and I didn't want to bring my bad mood into Crème de la Crêpe. I dressed, fed Beachley, and headed directly to the museum.

Although I was no longer in the mood for a tour of the dig site, I couldn't pass up the opportunity to learn something that might further my investigation. I made a mental note to meet up with Bernard Curtius to get some sleuthing pointers, and maybe find out if there'd been any news about Guy's murder investigation.

When I arrived at the museum, the guard was expecting me, and sent me right up to Marie's office.

Her door was open, but she was nowhere to be seen, so I sat down in her office and waited.

There was a cup of black coffee on her desk, as well as some travel brochures and a scuba diving magazine.

So we had something in common. I loved everything to do with the ocean—I could swim before I could walk—and I had my diving certification too. Maybe I could use this knowledge to break the ice if she got prickly again.

My eyes settled on the name plate on her desk: Marie Tremblay. I didn't know if *Tremblay* was a common name up here—like *Smith* or *Jones*—but Guy's antique store *was* Tremblay Antiques. I wondered again if they were related. Guy had described his ex-wife as cheating and two-faced. Marie hardly seemed to fit that description, but, then again, I'd only just met her.

Marie rushed in and dropped an armload of binders on her desk. "Sorry I'm late. Mornings are hectic around here. But I'm all yours now." She smiled, and this time it looked more sincere than during our last visit.

I was glad she was in a friendlier mood. Maybe it was a good time to ask about her name. "I notice your last name. Any relation to Tremblay Antiques?"

Her smile faded, and she sighed deeply. "Yes, I opened that store with my husband many years ago while working on my doctorate. That's why I wasn't so friendly yesterday. I'd just found out that he'd been murdered. Even though we've been apart for years, his death affected me deeply. There are still a lot of memories."

"It was a tragedy, for sure," I said gently. "He was an old friend of my family, and he was nice to me when I arrived. I thought we might even become friends."

Marie snorted and rolled her eyes. "Guy had no friends. I know it isn't good to speak of the dead this way, but his only true friend was money."

I wasn't entirely surprised by her words. Divorces were often acrimonious, particularly when large sums of money were involved. I remembered that Guy had said she was disloyal. Could an affair have broken up their marriage?

"He put his precious antiques before everything else," she continued, warming to her subject. "When I got this job, he began to treat me more like a competitor than a wife. He needed to get his hands on the best antiquities, no matter what the cost—even if it meant breaking the law."

She paused, as if suddenly aware that she'd said too much.

I was pleased with the direction our conversation was taking. It segued nicely into the topic I was hoping to discuss. Trying to sound as casual as possible, I asked, "Is there a black market for antiques?"

"Huge," she replied quickly. "A lot of artwork and antiquities are extremely valuable, and they're easy to steal with a bit of planning and timing. A lot of the biggest art thefts in history took place while museums were open to the public. But nowadays, museum security is getting a little better, so thieves are focusing more on soft targets like churches."

"I can't imagine that you've had problems with theft in this museum. There are cameras everywhere."

"Oh, we've had problems. Don't quote me on this, but things go missing all the time. Sometimes it's an employee taking advantage of bad record keeping. Other times it might be a crime of opportunity: a guard turns his head for a moment, an artifact is within arms reach, and voila! It's now floating around in the underworld."

I was fascinated. "So how do the thieves sell the artifacts? They can't just put them on EBay, right?"

"That's my point exactly," she said. "Anyone can steal. The hard part is the selling. You could use EBay or online marketplaces for artifacts the world has never seen before, but if the item is stolen, it's almost impossible to sell it without having connections."

I thought about the tapestry. Marie had mentioned that she'd never seen it before, and she was an expert. So it should be fairly easy for a thief to fence it without attracting much attention. I asked, "So how can one tell if an artifact was stolen?"

Marie settled back in her chair and narrowed her eyes suspiciously. "You seem to have a sudden interest in stolen artifacts. Any particular reason?"

Did I blow it? I didn't want her to know my tapestry

was missing. I wasn't sure why, but I felt it was a good idea to play my cards close to my vest. Two people were already dead, and if anything I said cost another person their life, I'd never forgive myself.

"No reason," I said casually. "It's just a fascinating topic. It reminds me of *The Thomas Crown Affair*, but it's even more exciting because this is the real thing."

It was a weak explanation, but I hoped that I'd sold her with my enthusiasm.

She smiled and nodded. "I like that movie too. I'm a sucker for anything with a museum in it. Anyway, if an artifact is stolen, it would appear in the Art Loss Register Database. There are over two hundred thousand items in it now."

I whistled, and she continued, "Stolen antiquities are a big business, right behind drug smuggling and the arms trade. To sell a stolen item, the thief would usually approach a museum or archaeology group that's known to acquire illegal items. Or he'd sell to a private collector or dealer. In these cases, they usually turn up fairly quickly. But unfortunately, stolen antiquities are often hidden until they cool off, or they're used as collateral for underworld drug deals, and are never seen again."

"Amazing," I said. "Thanks for telling me about all this. It sounds incredible."

"It's my pleasure. As you can tell, I like to talk about these things. Perhaps too much." She laughed lightly, and then stood. "I promised you a tour. I think you'll find that just as fascinating."

I smiled and followed her into the hall, wondering why she hadn't asked me about the tapestry. I'd promised to bring it for her to examine in person.

Did she already know it was missing?

Chapter 15

When we reached the boardwalk, Marie gave me an overview of the excavation.

Although I'd seen news segments about the dig and read about it in the newspapers, I was anxious to learn more from the lady who was overseeing the entire operation. And that was Marie.

"You probably heard of the last big project by Parks Canada a few years ago," she began, making an inclusive gesture around the wooden boardwalk where we stood. "All of this was torn up to give us access to the ruins of Chateau Saint-Louis, which burned to the ground almost a hundred years ago. They actually built this boardwalk over the top of it. The Chateau was the home of our governors for almost two hundred years. But during the excavation, we found remains of some even older buildings."

We walked in silence to the next location of my private tour. She'd switched into her public relations persona, probably out of habit. It made me want to keep my head down and my mouth shut like I was a kid on a class field trip.

We stopped in front of a metal and wood scaffolding that provided access up and over the railing of the boardwalk. Workers in grubby jeans and red hard hats were climbing up and down it on ladders, while others raised buckets on pulleys, and carefully poured the contents onto sorting tables.

Marie paused to give orders to a few passing workers before resuming her speech. "This is the dig site we started in the spring. This time, we had to work underneath the boardwalk instead of tearing it up. This was mostly due to the importance of our Funicular." She pointed to the iconic outdoor elevator that whisked tourists up and down the cliff separating the upper and lower parts of the old city.

One of the workers whom Marie spoke to ran up and handed us hard-hats, then smiled broadly and jogged back to his duties.

We put on our head protection while walking to the scaffolding.

"I'm going to show you something very exciting, Paul. We excavated a storeroom that was connected to the Chateau by a tunnel. It was very solidly built, so we think it was used originally for munitions storage. Later, it appears to have been used to store valuables and keep-sakes. Fortunately for us, the fire didn't get to them." She paused and looked at me seriously. "Please keep everything you see confidential. We don't want this getting out until we are ready to make a public announcement."

My imagination was going into overdrive. She was right; this was exciting! I could be one of the first to see something that had been sealed in time for centuries.

She paused to grab the rungs of a ladder and started to climb down. I followed cautiously, squeezing the rungs tightly. Everything I touched was covered in a layer of dust from the digging machinery, making the bars far too slippery for my liking.

When I saw the excavation, I felt a sense of wonder. It was much larger than I expected.

The boardwalk that soared above us was supported by enormous pillars that stretched two stories into the air. Tourists walking along the boardwalk above us cast shadows on the endless expanse of wooden planks. Huge high-pressure sodium lights lit up the dig site as effectively as the sun itself. Everywhere I looked, workers in yellow hats busied themselves in the dirt and rubble.

Marie raised her voice to be heard over the machinery. "We have three dozen laborers, plus field assistants, draftsmen and artifact experts." She pointed out the different areas of the excavation. "They're excavating the tunnel; the ones over there are working on the ice house, while our more experienced workers are tackling the storeroom itself."

I followed her to the storeroom, which proved to be about thirty feet square, with inner walls defining smaller areas that were probably side rooms or closets. The walls were all roughly the same height, and some still looked to be made of dirt since they hadn't been fully excavated yet.

Marie said, "The storeroom in front of you has a good deal of masonry around it, and it's a fairly large structure with high walls. We think it was used to store both weapons and the valuables of the governor and visiting dignitaries."

"You said it was intact. Where's the roof?"

"We removed it as we excavated for safety reasons, as well as to provide better access. Obviously, the roof doesn't serve much purpose now."

I nodded to show I understood.

We stopped and looked down into the trench, where a worker was scraping one of the storeroom's wall with a pointed trowel. "I believe you've already met Gaillard Duval," she said, whistling to get his attention.

When he saw us he grinned and waved like a schoolgirl. "Hello, Marie! Hi, Paul! I didn't expect to see you here!"

He dropped his trowel and looked around for something to wipe his hands on.

I was not really surprised to see him in designer

jeans and a white button-down shirt. He also wore a panama hat with a long peacock feather tucked in the band, and a gold diamond-crusted watch that sparkled as he moved. I wondered where he got his money, since the dig site was volunteer-based and the library presumably paid next to nothing.

We climbed down a short ladder to join him in the trench. "I like your work clothes," I said with a smile.

Gaillard exhaled noisily, but smiled. "I *know* you're not serious, Paul. I made a mistake wearing chiffon and we both know it. It wrinkles so easily."

I chuckled and explored Gaillard's work area, taking note of the tools of his trade. An assortment of shovels, brooms, dustpans, trowels, and picks were arranged around him. They were all dirty and well-used, except for a large pick-axe leaning against the wall. I grabbed the pick and turned it over in my hands. The wooden handle was well worn, but the sharp steel head looked brand new.

"Looks like this one doesn't get much use," I said.

"Why do you say that?" Gaillard asked.

"Well, it's clean. There isn't a speck on it. I thought it was strange, that's all."

Gaillard looked at the pick, and then at Marie. They both shrugged, then Gaillard took it from my hands and leaned it back against the wall. "Who knows, maybe an overeager student cleaned it."

I wondered why a student would go around cleaning dirty picks, but decided to drop the subject. I didn't want my gracious hosts to think I was some kind of idiot hung up on tools.

"So what have you found so far?" I asked.

Marie said, "At the previous dig site, we found mostly sherd, which is what we call small pieces of pottery, along with forks and some coins. But in this storeroom, we unearthed full sets of dishes and cutlery.

We've even found perfectly preserved eighteenth-century furniture. For the time period, most of it's of poor quality. But this was a settlement and there was really no place for luxuries. A few things were first-class, though. Remember that there were governors living here. Frontenac himself was a noble, and he had expensive tastes."

Gaillard laughed, "I read that he liked to be carried around on a litter."

Marie shot a glance at Gaillard. Apparently, she didn't like to be interrupted. "As I was saying, it was tradition for each new governor to acquire the furniture of his predecessor. So this building has yielded some spectacular items already, and may reveal more once we uncover the rest of the walls. Tell him about your recent find, Gaillard."

Gaillard put his hand in a large alcove in the wall, three feet in every dimension. "Last weekend when I excavated this wall, I found a magnificent wooden chest in this very spot. Very solid, but decaying—it's three hundred years old, so I suppose that's to be expected. Sadly, the lock was gone and the chest was empty. But we believe it once contained valuable heirlooms belonging to one of the governors, perhaps Frontenac himself! Take my word for it, it was a very significant find."

"You're like Indiana Jones!" I said. "Maybe you found the Lost Arc?"

"'Nothing shocks me. I'm a scientist'," Gaillard quoted, in a what I assumed was an impression of Harrison Ford doing a line from the movie.

Marie rolled her eyes and looked at her watch. "I have to head back to the office; I've shown you everything of importance. You're welcome to remain here for awhile if you like, Paul."

"I appreciate it. Thank you for the tour. It was

amazing."

Marie hurried away with her phone held to her ear, and I turned back to Gaillard. "All of these artifacts must be worth a fortune. You should have armed guards standing next to you."

"What's that supposed to mean?" Gaillard asked.

Time for damage control. I acted as though I was horror-struck for being misunderstood. "I didn't mean that someone should keep an eye on you. I meant in the same way you have guards standing near the door in banks, to discourage thieves. I was just making a bad joke; I apologize."

Gaillard visibly relaxed. "No, I'm the one who should be sorry. Everyone's on edge lately because artifacts are missing from the dig and the museum. And yes, we do have security after hours."

This was the chance I was waiting for.

"How could someone take something from the dig? I assume detailed records are kept."

Gaillard showed me a clipboard and a plastic bag. "Oh yes, very detailed. When an item is found, no matter how small it is, we bag it and assign it an artifact number. It doesn't matter if it's a single coin or a tiny fragment of china. Everything is described and placed in one of these bags, then the bag goes into a bucket. When the buckets are full, they're taken away."

"Taken away?"

"We bring them to the basement of the museum for cleaning and analysis, then put them in drawers for Marie to examine in more detail."

I stooped down to examine the contents of his bucket. It was half filled with plastic sample bags, and each bag contained a dirty scrap of metal or a sherd.

"A lot of this looks like clumps of dirt," I admitted. "You must have a good eye."

"There are tricks of the trade that you learn over

time. If you see a glimmer of green, it's usually a coin. If you see something white, it might be a fragment of pottery or bone. And if you think it's bone, you can test it by putting it on your tongue. If it sticks, it's bone."

"Blah," I said with a grimace. "Why would there be pieces of bone? Did the settlers bury their dead here?"

"No, it's typically food scraps—animal bones and fish bones. A lot of what we find is old garbage. There's a lot of organic soil here which suggests vegetables and meat. They didn't have curb-side pickup like we do today."

"So if a thief wanted to help himself to something," I began, "he'd have to do it before it gets assigned an artifact number. Maybe stick it in his pocket when nobody was looking."

Gaillard looked uncomfortable but managed a weak smile. "Something like that. You should get going, the site supervisor is around and I want to look busy. It was nice seeing you, Paul."

I thanked him and returned to the scaffolding.

As I climbed up the ladder, I noticed something that I hadn't seen on the way down. A narrow path led from the dig site into the trees along the side of the cliff.

I shielded my eyes from the sun and squinted down the path. I could just make out yellow police tape flapping in the breeze.

It was the site of Remy's murder.

Chapter 16

Once I was safely back on top of the boardwalk, I took a moment to appreciate my surroundings. Until now, my time in the old city had been anything but relaxing. I had to steal these moments whenever I could.

Standing at the iron railing, I lost myself in the splendor of the Saint Laurence River. The sun danced on the waves and created a million tiny flashes of light.

A wise person once said that if you are ever lonely, you should go to the water because it will always wave back.

A cruise-ship had pulled up while I was visiting the dig site below. A steady stream of tourists was marching from the ship to the shops facing the river like ants to a sandwich. I heard their distant voices and laughter on the wind. I suddenly felt very far from home.

I walked back to my building, feeding off the energy from a new batch of tourists pouring into the city for the weekend. Not in any rush to get back, I stopped to enjoy every street performer I passed and gave each a generous tip.

As soon as I got home, I collapsed into a chair in my air-conditioned kitchen and punched Francine's number into my phone. She answered on the tenth ring, just as I was preparing to hang up.

"Hello?" she said, sounding exhausted.

"Hey, it's me—Paul."

She seemed to perk up a little. "Oh, hi, Paul. How

are you?"

"Actually, I was calling to see how you were." I didn't want to mention Remy, in case she hadn't heard the news yet.

"I've had better days," she said, choking up. "I assume you know about Remy. I'm still in shock."

"Yes, I know. I really am sorry. I wish I'd had more time to get to know him. He seemed very nice."

"Thanks; he was."

"Well, listen, I owe you a dinner. Would you like to go out tonight?"

"I'm afraid I wouldn't be good company tonight, Paul."

"Don't worry about that. We can talk about anything you like, or we can just sit quietly and eat. Whatever you need."

The line went silent for a few moments. "Alright; maybe I could use a distraction. I can stop by this evening. I need to do a test fitting of your costume, anyway."

"Perfect. See you tonight."

I hung up the phone just as Bernard appeared outside my front door. He was holding up two paper bags with a huge grin on his face.

Assuming it was something tasty, I rushed to let him in.

"I hope you haven't eaten yet," Bernard said. "I brought the national dish of Quebec!"

We went to the kitchen and Bernard removed Styrofoam boxes and plastic cutlery from the bags, along with a couple of frosty beers.

"The poutine is from Vladamir's Poutine, a few doors down. The beers are from Bernard's."

"What is Bernard's, a liquor store?" I asked.

"I'm Bernard. They're from my place, dummy."

I tore open my box and examined the delightful,

gooey contents. There were golden French fries and melted cheddar cheese curds. Everything was smothered in rich steaming gravy. "Yum, the smell is out of this world. And not just because I'm starving."

Bernard said, "I also got one of Vlad's new menu items: fries with herbs, grated cheese, hollandaise sauce, and a poached egg. We can trade if you like, I thought you might like a choice."

"Not on your life," I said. "I'll stick with the classic. Let's eat."

I made sure to get copious amounts of each artery-clogging ingredient onto my fork before shoveling it into my mouth. It was so good that I wondered how a meal could possibly be better.

Then I remembered how. I cracked open a beer and gulped half of it down.

"Wow," Bernard said, "When was the last time you ate?"

"I've had a lot of sugary things this week. I guess my body was starving for some proper nutrition."

Bernard filled his mouth with fries and hollandaise. "Don't kid yourself. This is probably the most unhealthy meal on the planet."

"Come on, it's full of carbohydrates and protein. There's some good stuff in here!" I took another large bite while eyeing my food with suspicion.

"Nope. It's a heart attack on a plate, my friend. It'll kill you," Bernard said between bites and sips of beer.

We continued to eat in silence, then we tossed our empty containers in the garbage and finished our beers.

We relaxed for a few minutes, giving our poutine stupor a chance to wear off. Bernard said, "I'd be happy to fix your lock, if you like."

"Thanks, but I don't want to trouble you. I'll call a locksmith."

"Are you crazy? They'll charge hundreds of dollars

and sell you things you don't need. I can buy you a lock at the hardware store and install it in no time flat."

"Shouldn't I use a commercial quality lock?" I asked.

"Listen, as an ex-cop I've seen a lot of break-ins. If someone wants to get in, they're getting in. Locks are pretty much all the same."

I shrugged. "That reminds me. Have you heard anything about the antique store murder from your police contacts? Or is that classified information?"

"They're being pretty tight-lipped about it. They haven't made any arrests yet, but they seem to be focusing their investigation on Napoleon, and Guy's ex-wife."

"What would Napoleon's motive be?"

"Besides being a nut job? There's a lot of history between those two. Guy took Napoleon Roy on as an equal partner when he was starting his antique store and needed capital. Over the years, Napoleon made some bad investments, and ended up selling his shares in the business to Guy—a little here, a little there—until his fifty percent stake shrank to fifteen. Even though it was Napoleon's own fault for cashing out his shares, he never could get over the fact that he missed out on millions of dollars."

"So they think the murder was a crime of passion?"

"That, and opportunity. Guy and Napoleon had an agreement where Napoleon gets all of Guy's shares in the event of his death, and vice versa. That means Napoleon takes over Guy's share of the business now. Who knows, maybe when Guy sold you the building, it finally pushed Napoleon over the edge since he'd always figured it would be his one day. I don't think Guy ever intended to give that building to Napoleon, but he dangled it like a carrot to keep him around—Napoleon did a lot of free work on the building, and he's important to the antique store."

"So what about Marie's motive?"

Bernard looked surprised. "How did you know that Marie is Guy's ex?"

"I figured it out when I recognized the last name on her door. She confirmed that they were divorced."

"They weren't divorced," Bernard said, "just legally separated. According to Guy's financial records, he was paying her a huge monthly alimony, then all of a sudden, the payments stopped. So Landry figures she might have killed him out of anger. Or she might have killed him for his money. Either way, she gets it all now."

"But you said Napoleon gets everything?"

"The partnership agreement stipulated that Napoleon gets Guy's shares in the *business*. But Guy's other assets and cash—which are considerable—go to Marie."

Like the poutine, this was a lot to digest. My head was pounding, and I was beginning to miss my carefree surf days.

Bernard said, "I have to get going, but I'll be back later to fix that lock."

"You don't mind?"

"Not at all. I can do it tonight after work. I'll bring you a receipt from the hardware store. But no charge for the labor."

I was touched. "You're a saint, Bernard."

"I haven't heard that one before," Bernard said with a smile, then clapped me on the back and got up to leave.

I scribbled my phone number on a fragment of one of the takeout bags, and handed it to him. "Just in case you need to reach me. I'm going out with Francine from the costume store, so I might not see you tonight. She was a good friend of the man who was killed last night, so she could use some cheering up."

Bernard winked and went out the door.

It was time to get some serious work done.

I fired up my computer to design my storefront sign. I chose a decorative, old style font that captured the ambiance of a wax museum, and created the text in heavy black letters against a white background. When I was satisfied with the results on the screen, I printed the text in actual size on standard sheets of paper.

I spread a plastic tarp on the floor, and laid the old wax museum sign on it, upside down. The back of the sign was in pristine shape. It was already painted glossy white, and it had not discolored over the years since the back of the sign had been shielded from the sun and weather.

I layered the printed pages over the sign board with tracing paper, then traced the outlines of the letters. Then with a steady hand, I filled in all the letters using the paint and brushes I'd bought at the local hardware store.

I stood back and admired my work. The end result looked very professional. Best of all, I saved myself the time and expense of buying a sign, which could have cost thousands of dollars.

The process had taken all afternoon, and it was growing dark outside.

I changed into my best clothes and freshened up for my dinner with Francine. Just as I came down the stairs feeling like a new man, Francine let herself in through the front door.

"Woo-wee! I like your outfit," I exclaimed. Without her glasses and with her hair straightened, she looked years younger than I thought she was when we'd met. In fact, we looked to be the same age, and she was surprisingly attractive.

She twirled dramatically, then stumbled over the new sign.

"Are you okay?" I asked.

"Just embarrassed," Francine said, blushing while she surveyed my handiwork. "You've been busy! Did you paint this yourself?"

"Yeah, just now."

"I like the font. It makes the museum seem mysterious and exciting."

"Thanks. That was the idea."

Francine looked over my newly-stocked shelves and made sounds of approval as she poked through the consignment items on loan from Old Fashion. She seemed to like the mannequins I'd put together too, but she laughed when she saw the footwear. "The high-heels belong to the man's costume, believe it or not."

I thought Francine accidentally sent me only women's footwear, so the male mannequin was wearing a pair of my flip-flops.

"I hope nobody expects me to wear heels at the festival," I said, still staring at the shoes.

She placed a sheet of paper on the counter and smiled. "I'm surprised you're wearing shoes right now, to be honest. Anyway, I brought a price sheet for you. It's just a guide; the final decision is up to you, of course."

"Great, and thanks again. It's hard to fill all these shelves—I thought I might take some of them down."

"I wouldn't. Sometimes less is more. It makes each item seem more special when it has space around it. Oh, I brought your costume." She produced a frilly shirt and pants from a wardrobe bag. "It isn't finished yet, but it will be in a few days. I just want to check the sizing. I'm usually pretty good at measuring, so it should be perfect."

She handed me the pants and covered her eyes with her hands. "You can change here; I won't look."

I grinned and changed my pants, keeping my eyes focused on her hands the entire time. She left a crack between her fingers to peek through.

"That's odd," I said, as I tried to fasten the pants.

Francine lowered her hands and examined my waistline. "Hmm... It looks like I was off by a few inches on your waistline. That's never happened before."

I sucked in my stomach and tried in vain to do up the button. I noticed with horror that my once flat stomach now felt soft and pudgy. "Yep. I guess you blew it with the measuring."

She narrowed her eyes and smiled. 'Or maybe it's too many French treats!" She poked me in the stomach.

We laughed, then Francine had me try on the shirt, with similar results.

"I can let them out," she said. "We leave a lot of extra fabric in the seams so that they can be altered for rentals, since we can't afford to keep too many sizes in stock. Just try not to get any bigger before next week, okay?"

I saluted. "I promise to start eating right," I paused. "After tonight."

"Sounds good," she said. "I'm starving, so I'm not letting you get away with buying salads tonight."

I switched off the lights and we stepped out into the cool night air. Across the street, I saw Sophie in Crème de la Crêpe wiping down a table near the window. I was strangely relieved that she didn't seem to notice us, even though we were just two friends going out for dinner.

We strolled along the restaurants of Rue Ste. Anne, each of which had an attractive menu girl standing in the doorway to draw in customers. Most of the restaurants had their windows thrown open to the sidewalk so customers could enjoy the fresh air. Swatting flies seemed to be a price they were happy to pay for ringside seats.

"Do you have a preference?" Francine asked.

"Actually, I made reservations at Saint-Ardeur."

Her eyes widened. "No, Paul. It's far too expensive. I was only kidding earlier; I'd be happy with a burger."

"Sorry, you said it was my choice. I'm holding you to it."

"Okay, you win. But let me get the tip," she said.

"We'll see."

When we rounded a corner, I saw something that made me stop dead in my tracks.

Chapter 17

"Is that Gaillard Duval?" I whispered.

We stood in front of a cozy little restaurant with striped awnings and hanging flowers. The sun had fallen below the horizon, and the windows shone like gold against the indigo sky. In a corner booth next to the window, a couple was enjoying a romantic meal by candlelight. The man was almost certainly Gaillard Duval since smarmy curled up moustaches were so rare in the this century. The lady was sitting very close with her head on his shoulder. They looked like a photo in a cheesy heart-shaped locket.

I was shocked when I noticed that it was Marie Tremblay from the Settlement Museum.

Francine followed my gaze and squinted, but she didn't share my astonishment. "Yes, that's him. So what?"

I took her hand and rushed her past the restaurant so we wouldn't be spotted. "Well, there are a few things wrong with that scene. First, he's having dinner with Marie Tremblay. He works for her, and there's a significant age difference."

"Oh, that," Francine said. "Age is not so important in Quebec. You often see young ladies and older men together. And occasionally, vice-versa. What else do you find unusual?"

I tried to make my next point delicately. "Well, I thought he preferred the company of other *men*."

She laughed. "Gaillard is not gay, just French! I know it's hard to tell the difference sometimes; We're a

fashionable people. But I've seen him with older
women before, ones he met while working at Tremblay
Antiques last summer. I can't believe you thought
that!"

I was troubled. Maybe I needed to add Gaillard
Duval to my list of murder suspects? He could have
killed Guy to ensure Marie's financial future, and, in a
roundabout way, to support his own lavish lifestyle. Or
maybe Gaillard and Marie were conspirators?

We resumed our walk to the restaurant. Francine
walked so close to me that our hands and arms brushed
together. She seemed a little unsteady with her heels on
the cobblestones, so I linked my arm in hers and said, "I
don't want you to fall."

She just smiled. By the time we reached Saint
Ardeur, Francine seemed to be her old self again. When
I held the door open for her, I couldn't help but wonder
if we were on a date.

The *maître d'* showed us to our table in a large
indoor conservatory with a glass ceiling several stories
high. We were surrounded by vivid stained glass
panels, rich gleaming wood, and polished brass. Tiny
twinkling lights seemed to float in the air. I wasn't sure
if the stars outside or the crystal light fixtures were
creating the effect. Either way, the room was magical,
and Francine looked as impressed as I felt.

Francine said, "I've lived here for two years and
have never stepped inside this place. I had no idea it
was this beautiful."

"If the food is half as great as the decor, we're in for
a real treat!" I said.

We looked over our menus. Francine shook her head
and looked at me over her menu. "It all looks so good!"

I closed my menu and a waiter approached our table.
"Why don't you order for both of us?" I suggested. "I'll
have whatever you have. I'm sure everything is

incredible."

"You got it." She gave the waiter our order, and we shared a bottle of wine while waiting for our food.

I decided to test the waters and ask about Remy, in case she wanted to talk. "So where did you meet Remy?"

She stared into her wine glass. "We met in our last year of university in Montreal. I was a history student and took theatre and dance. Remy had to take a history course to fulfil his graduation requirements."

"You mentioned that he made some bad decisions," I said.

"Yes, he started to get mixed up with some actors who used drugs. After graduation, I convinced him to get an apartment with me here. He was like a little brother to me, and he was a lot of fun to be around when he wasn't getting into mischief." She paused to sip her wine, then fidgeted with the glass. "Everything was going fine after that. He became a busker to earn money, and he got very good at it. He'd make hundreds of dollars a day sometimes. Lately, he was trying out a new act where he'd dress up as a bronze statue. He was trying different things to see where he could make the most money."

"So it sounds like things were going well. Why did he move out?"

"On moving day he decided he wanted to be on his own, and that was that."

"What do you mean by moving day?" I asked.

"The first of July. Just about everyone in Quebec moves on that date. We call it *the restless feet*. I guess Remy got them. It's in our blood."

"When was the last time you were in contact with him?"

"This past weekend. He said he was going to be rich." She rolled her eyes and smiled faintly.

A passing waitress refilled our glasses.

"You're welcome to sort through Remy's things if you want," I said. "It sounds like you're the closest thing he had to family. But there's no rush; you can take all the time you need."

When she didn't reply, I decided it was a good time to steer the conversation away from Remy. I told her about my life back in Vancouver, and she talked about the city and the upcoming festival. The conversation flowed easily until our food arrived.

We started with a rich and velvety lobster bisque, and succulent crab cakes covered in a tangy sweet corn puree. This was followed by a rack of lamb with a balsamic sauce so delicious I was tempted to lick my plate. For dessert, we had raspberry crème brulée and strong Venetian coffee with whipped cream.

As we basked in the afterglow of a perfect meal, my cell phone snapped me back to reality.

"It's a text from Bernard Curtius. He says my new keys are in the flower pot." I switched off my phone and sighed. "What a meal!"

"It was spectacular," she agreed. "Worth every penny you spent."

I took care of the bill and we stepped out into the cool night air.

"We can part ways here if you like," Francine said, "We're heading in separate directions."

"Don't be silly, I'm taking you home. I'm looking forward to burning off a few calories."

She raised an eyebrow, and I realized my words could be taken two ways.

"I meant by walking," I explained with a sheepish grin, "Not at your apartment."

When we reached her front door, we found it hanging open. "Someone's been here."

Francine charged into her living room with a look of

disbelief, and then anger. She moved from room to room, taking a mental inventory of her possessions. Then she exhaled. "Well that's a relief; nothing's missing."

"But the place is trashed!" I exclaimed.

She shook her head. "No, if anything, they cleaned it up."

I chuckled nervously, but felt no real humor in the situation. I was going to have to pick up the pace on my investigation before anyone else I cared about was hurt.

"I admire your courage," I said.

"I'm just numb. It'll take more than this to erase the dinner we just had." Tears appeared in her eyes. "Thanks for tonight, I needed that. I need to be alone now; I hope you understand."

I gave her a reassuring hug and slipped quietly out the front door.

As I walked home, I wondered how many people knew about her connection to Remy. Gaillard certainly did, thanks to library records. And Napoleon probably knew because he was the former superintendent of my building, and Francine Chapelle was probably listed as a reference on Remy's rental application. As for Marie, well, I supposed she could have looked in an old phone book, or gotten the information from Gaillard.

But I had one big question.

Why was the thief still searching for the tapestry that he'd presumably stolen from my building the previous day? It didn't make any sense. Maybe Francine's break-in had nothing to do with me, or my tapestry?

Back at my building, I found my front door locked with a shiny new deadbolt. I dug my key out of the flower pot and let himself in.

After the excitement of the day and the calorie rich dinner, I could barely keep my eyes open as I greeted Beachley and trudged upstairs to bed.

As my final act of the day, I sent a text to Dottie:
*Looking forward to your return, Watson. We have a
case to solve.*

Chapter 18

Crème de la Crêpe was jammed with customers when I arrived for breakfast.

Suzie, the restaurant manager, was assisting the crepe girls behind the counter. I was dismayed to see that all of the stools were occupied.

"Hi, Paul!" Suzie called out over the clamor. "Sophie has the morning off. There's a booth available by the window if you like."

I was surprised that she knew my name. I flashed her a smile. "No thanks, I'll just get a dozen pastries and eat at home. I should get an early start today."

"That's some breakfast," she joked, folding a box for my order. "What can I get for you?"

"How about some chocolate éclairs, blueberry lollies, and chocolate pops. Oh, and maybe some of those brownies and lemon polenta cakes."

If Dottie and I were going to solve a mystery, then, by golly, we would need fuel. And I'd better have extra on hand, in case my portly friend from next door dropped in.

Suzie rang up my order and handed over a large box neatly wrapped in a bow. "We'll try to save you a seat tomorrow. It gets crazy around here on weekends."

I thanked her and rushed home to put the water on to boil.

Dottie arrived a few minutes later, immediately noticing the new sign on the floor. "Oh, Paul, that's excellent. Much better than the original sign. I know it will be great for business." She glanced around the store. "The shelves are full of stock too! You've been busy."

The kettle whistled and we went to the kitchen to prepare our coffee. When she saw the large box of pastries on the table, she looked surprised. "Are we going to eat all these? Good thing I didn't have breakfast."

"Solving a murder is hungry work," I said, "Besides, going to the crêperie gives me a chance to see a girl I like."

"Oh, really? Which one?"

"Her name is Sophie."

"Sophie?" Dottie seemed pleased and surprised. "Bless her heart. She's a sweet kid. It sounds like you're really fond of her."

"Sure am. I'm playing it cool though. I don't even know if she's single."

"I've never seen her with anyone in the time that I've known her, but you never know," Dottie said with a wink.

She poured coffee and cream into our mugs and I spooned brown sugar into mine. We each selected a few pastries from the box.

We sipped our coffee in silence, enjoying the first caffeine of the day.

"So," Dottie began. "I'm pleased to hear that you've taken an interest in Guy's murder and want my help. I'm a fan of detective stories, as you know."

"Well, we have a real doozey on our hands. Wait until you hear what you've missed."

"Hold that thought," Dottie said. She bent over and rummaged through her bag, and reappeared from underneath the table wearing a deerstalker hat and a Sherlock Holmes pipe.

Anyone else would have concluded that Dottie had a screw loose, but I was an eccentric person myself. I laughed and held up a hand in mock protest. "Wait! Shouldn't Sherlock get to wear that?"

"She is. But don't worry, I brought something for you too." She handed me my own hat and pipe.

I put them on, took a pretend puff, and coughed. "Okay. As I was saying, a lot has happened since you were gone."

I described the events of the past few days, while Dottie listened with rapt attention.

When I told her about Remy's murder, her eyes grew to twice their normal size behind her thick glasses. Then when I told her about the Gobelin tapestry, her eyes grew larger still, and the plastic pipe hung down from her gaping mouth.

"You mean that filthy old rug is worth a million buckaroos?" she exclaimed.

"Maybe more, who knows? The thing is, I can't figure out how all of this ties together."

Dottie said, "Well, to begin with, it's fairly obvious that the tapestry spent the last three centuries in that old chest they dug up. They're both from the same time period, and they both came to light in the last week."

I was impressed. Why didn't I connect those dots? I could have been standing next to a murderer yesterday, recklessly asking questions about fencing stolen artifacts from the dig site. Real smooth, Paul. I swore to be more careful in the future—mistakes like that could get someone killed.

"We're making progress already," I said. "So to summarize, we have two murder victims and one stolen tapestry. We know where it was taken from, but we don't know by whom. We also don't know how it came into Remy's possession."

Dottie took a slow sip of her coffee and smiled like she'd swallowed a canary. "I'm afraid that isn't entirely accurate, Paul."

She paused for drama, and made a big show of blowing on her coffee. "It relates to your priceless tapestry." Blow, blow. "The one which appears to lie at the heart of our mystery..."

She had my full attention now.

"The tapestry is in my trunk."

I jumped to my feet. "I can't believe it! What's it doing there?"

"I was planning to get it dry-cleaned, along with the curtains, so I just took it."

I sat down in shock, and popped a miniature cupcake in my mouth while I considered the implications. "Wow. I guess that changes everything."

"Not necessarily," Dottie said, freshening up our coffees. "You said there was a break-in here *and* another one at Francine's apartment. So it appears that someone is *still* searching for something. If I hadn't put the tapestry in my trunk, it might very well have been stolen by now anyway."

"Hmm. Good point." I was starting to think I stunk at investigating. "Give me a minute to think."

Dottie inhaled deeply from her plastic pipe, leaned back, and did an impression of a fish gulping for air.

"What's that supposed to be?" I asked.

"I'm blowing smoke rings."

"I've never seen Sherlock Holmes make smoke rings," I said, jabbing the stem of my pipe towards her. "Or Watson, for that matter."

"Don't all pipe smokers make rings? I thought that was the whole point."

"Beats me," I said, taking a pretend puff.

"You remember that cat from Alice in Wonderland?" I asked, "The one with the big teeth? He made some kick-ass rings with his pipe. Spelled letters, too."

"It was a hookah," Dottie corrected.

"Are you sure? I could have sworn it was a cat."

"No, Paul, the cat was a caterpillar. The pipe was a hookah."

I flailed my arms in frustration. "Never mind. We need to focus."

Just then, Dottie turned her head to the doorway and I followed her gaze. Bernard was leaning against the frame with his arms crossed and an eyebrow raised, smiling ear to ear.

"The criminals of Quebec can sleep easy with you two on the case," he quipped. "Oh, and nice hats. Mind if I pull up a chair?"

"Please do," I said. I pushed the box of baked goods in front of an empty seat.

Bernard poured himself a coffee and flopped down. "I just stopped by to see how the new lock is working out?"

"No problems so far. And thanks again; I owe you one."

"Don't mention it," he said, helping himself to a pastry puff. "I was planning on leaving it unlocked and putting the key on your counter, but that clown Napoleon came by." He took a bite of his pastry, closed his eyes and smiled. "Man, this is good."

I said, "That Napoleon is getting on my last nerve. What did he want?"

"You're not going to believe this. He pulled up with a pick-up truck and was planning to clean out your museum and shop. I practically had to throw him out."

My blood started to boil. "Go on."

"He said everything belongs to him now because it originally came from Tremblay Antiques, and due to a death clause in their partnership agreement, he takes over Guy's share of the business."

I glanced at Dottie. She seemed angry too, or at least as angry as a person can look with a toy Sherlock

Holmes' pipe in her mouth.

"It's a good thing you changed the locks!" I said. "That Napoleon is a real piece of work."

"I've met worse," Bernard said, sucking the cream from an éclair. "Anyway, I let it slip that you'd gone out for dinner with Francine. Then it occurred to me that he might try to come back after I left."

Dottie said, "You're a good man, Bernard. Thank you."

Bernard got up to leave. "Sorry I can't stay, folks. Don't forget to invite me to your next detective meeting. Just say the word *éclair* and I'll drop everything!"

He winked and went out the front door.

When he was out of sight, Dottie's smile faded. "I hope you don't invite him to our next meeting, Paul. That man is about as sharp as mashed potatoes."

"No way; it's just you and me," I said, returning to my seat. "Now, as I was saying, we have three separate crimes here. Guy's murder, Remy's murder, and the theft of a tapestry from the dig site. Let's assume for now that they're all connected."

"Agreed," Dottie said.

"The chain of events begins with the tapestry being dug up on the weekend. Several days later, Guy is murdered, then Remy a few days after that. Remy believed he was coming into a large sum of money, and the tapestry was hidden right here in this building. Someone broke in and searched this building, and then they ransacked Francine's apartment yesterday, probably knowing about her relationship to Remy."

Dottie gasped. "Francine was broken into too? That's awful! I guess the killer is still searching for the tapestry."

"Right. So why kill Guy and Remy?"

Dottie said, "Let's simplify the problem and start

with Guy's murder. He was a nice man, rest his soul, but he was ruthless in business. A man doesn't get that successful that quickly without bending a few rules."

I nodded. "When I was talking to Marie at the museum, she all but admitted that Guy had purchased black market antiquities."

"I don't know about that," Dottie said. "I've been doing his taxes for the past twenty years. I did them for the wax museum, and I do them today for his antique store. I haven't seen anything in his bank statements that I would call proof of criminal activity. But I wouldn't put it past that horrible partner of his."

"Yeah, Napoleon," I moaned. "Guy did tell me that Napoleon had a knack for acquiring rare items. At the time, it sounded like is was alluding to something illegal. Maybe the killer knew that Tremblay Antiques had acquired the tapestry, and tried to steal it, and Guy got killed during the robbery?"

"Or what if the killer and the person who excavated the tapestry are the same person?" Dottie asked. "He could have tried to sell it to Guy. Then Guy either blackmailed him or ripped him off."

I drummed my fingers on the table. "Interesting. But how did Remy get his hands on it?"

"Good question," Dottie said. "This is a real dilly! Trying to solve a real life mystery is a lot different than reading a book."

I nodded thoughtfully. "A mystery is like a wave in the ocean. It looks simple, but it contains hidden secrets and patterns that most people don't see. The secret is to look, to really see the sea."

"Oh, for crying out loud, Paul!" Dottie exclaimed.

I chuckled. It was fun pushing Dottie's buttons. "Okay, let's try looking at this from another angle. Who removed the tapestry from the chest?"

"Well, who are our main suspects?"

"It must have been Gaillard. He was the first to dig up the chest. He said that it was empty when he opened it, but he could have removed the tapestry himself and thrown away the lock, if there even was one."

"How do you know he was the first to dig it up?"

I tilted my head. "You know, I hadn't thought of that. Marie did mention that she works at the site, too. She has full access to the dig site, even after hours. She could have found the chest, then covered it back up after she stole the tapestry."

"That's using the old bean!" Dottie exclaimed, "Who do you think is more likely between the two of them?"

"Marie has too much to lose, so I'd guess Gaillard. He has expensive tastes for a part-time archaeologist. He wore a diamond-studded Rolex to the dig site."

Dottie asked, "Maybe he has a benefactor? Does he have any family?"

"All I know is that he lived in France and relocated here just over a year ago. Maybe Marie is buying him gifts? I saw them looking real cozy at a restaurant last night."

"Well, I'm leaning towards Marie," Dottie said. "If our tapestry thief and killer are the same person, then she has a motive for both crimes. She and Guy had some violent fights, and she gave as good as she got. She'd have been in the best position to sell the tapestry for maximum profit using her connections. It isn't listed as stolen, so she could get a very high price for it on the open market."

I admired Dottie's loyalty to Guy, but we needed to consider every possibility. "Or, she might have tried to sell it to Guy, and then he decided to blackmail her instead of paying for it. Or maybe they were working together, and she got greedy and killed him."

There was one key element missing from all our

theories: Remy's murder. How did he fit into the puzzle?

Chapter 19

"So where do we go from here?" Dottie asked, draining her cup.

"I'm not sure. Why don't we work while we think it over? I concentrate best when my hands are busy."

I grabbed a few chocolates on my way out of the kitchen and signaled for Beachley to follow us. If I was going to be spending so much time in the basement, I wanted her to get used to hanging out there instead of upstairs by herself in front of the fireplace.

At the top of the stairs, I turned and faced Dottie. "I was thinking. Maybe we should just give the customers what they want after all, and make a Celine Dion and Rocket Richard exhibit? I can't imagine anyone wanting to pose for family pictures next to a screaming man with severed hands."

Dottie's eyes lit up. "Gee, that sounds like fun! I'll choose a few figures that are the right height and weight. There are some old sequin dresses in my scrap material bin that I can alter."

"Cool. The Rocket should be the easier of the two. We just need to pick out a figure with the right facial shape, and give him some bushy eyebrows and a *Canadiens* jersey."

"You got it, boss."

"How are you doing on the Étienne Brule exhibit?" I asked.

"Oh, I finished it already. So I can get started on the new figures right away."

I couldn't wait to see the finished exhibit. I flicked

on the basement lights and rushed down the stairs, followed closely by Dottie and Beachley.

The exhibit was even better than I'd envisioned. The creepy atmospheric music, combined with cool lighting and Dottie's mad modelling skills, really brought the gruesome diorama to life. Poor Étienne Brule was having a bad time of it. Lashed to a tree stump, his body was contorted in unspeakable agony, and his wild eyes looked on as an Indian warrior held a nasty-looking knife to his chest. Both of his severed hands, and one of his feet, were roasting over an open fire. The other foot was being eaten by an Indian woman and her child, who munched on either end like it was a scene from *Lady and the Tramp*.

All I could think of while I looked at it was, *too bad it wasn't Todd*.

I stood back and soaked it all in. "This exhibit is mint, Dottie. The difference between this exhibit and the others is like night and day. If we do 'em all up like this, someone might actually be willing to pay admission." I held my hand up in front of her. "High Five!"

"I don't do high fives," she said.

"You don't do high fives?" I repeated in disbelief. "What the flip? You can't just leave me hanging."

"Oh, yes I can. It's too risky. It won't come off right and I'll look foolish."

I laughed. "It's just the two of us here. If it doesn't go well, it'll be our little secret."

"Don't be a pill."

"Listen, Dottie. You did an awesome job, so it'd be a tragedy if we didn't high five. Come on, take a chance! Do it for me."

I waited while she mulled it over.

"Oh, honest to Pete!" she exclaimed. Then she swung her hand up at the precise moment that I'd given up hope and was lowering mine. What came next was a perfect storm of slow reflexes and poor coordination, ending with her hand getting snagged in my hair.

Dottie didn't look amused.

I broke the silence. "That was the most bogus high five *ever*."

"Precisely as I imagined it would go," Dottie said bitterly. "Now be a good boy and pass me those long scissors."

"Only if you're planning to cut your hand off like Étienne over there. My hair is staying right where it is." I untangled her hand from my glorious mane, then squatted down next to Beachley.

"High five, buddy!" I said, holding my hand up.

Beachley raised her front paw and touched my hand with it.

Dottie exhaled loudly and held her head in her hands. "Someone should blister your cakes, Paul. We need to get back to work. Are we planning to open the museum for the festival?"

"That's the plan," I said. "I'm going to do a quick mini-makeover of as many exhibits as I can. I'd rather spend the time we have left improving all of the exhibits a small amount, rather than creating just one more great exhibit."

"Do you need any help?"

"Naw, you just go ahead and work on Celine. I'm going to go through these displays one at a time, cleaning and tweaking them. Maybe I'll add some sound tracks here and there, and print out some backgrounds with my new printer. If I need any help with the costumes, I'll come get you."

"Come on, Beachley," Dottie said. "I know a nice place where you can sleep." Beachley trudged along behind her and they disappeared into the office. A few minutes later, I heard a sewing machine.

Some of the exhibits weren't too bad and only needed to be dusted. Others had small issues that could be easily fixed such as armatures peaking out from under their clothing, or badly painted scenery visible through fake windows. The latter I could replace by printing out background scenes on my new printer.

I limited myself to one hour per exhibit. I didn't want to spend too much time on them since they'd likely be replaced in the next few months. I worked enthusiastically for several hours, and finished all of the displays on one side of the corridor.

Just as I was getting hungry, Dottie emerged from the office. She looked tired but had a big smile on her face. "I've made some good progress on our celebrities. I found some wax figures that would make a perfect Celine and Rocket. I'm using your office as a workroom; I hope you don't mind."

"Not at all; I won't be using that room as my office any time soon. You can consider it your own private waxworks for now."

"Thank you, Paul," she said. "By the way, I'm heading home to have lunch. Would you like to come along?"

"Really? You bet. It'll be nice to eat something that isn't made of sugar. Are you sure it's no problem?"

"Heavens, no! You can meet my granddaughter."

We went upstairs, shutting the lights off behind us. I didn't want to show up at Dottie's empty-handed, so I searched my store shelves for a suitable child's gift, and settled on a package of temporary tattoos of the Quebec flag.

When Dottie looked at me curiously, I said, "A present for your granddaughter."

She smiled and we stepped outside into the bright sunlight. I had to squint until my eyes adjusted. It was dark in the museum; I still hadn't remembered to replace the burnt-out bulbs.

Dottie suddenly changed direction and headed down a side street, motioning for me to follow. "We're taking a little detour. I've got an idea."

I could tell right away that she was leading me to the library.

"Hang on," I called after her, as I struggled to keep up. "Where are we going? We need to think before we act."

"Oh, horse feathers! Do you hesitate when you're facing one of those big waves you keep going on about?"

She had me there. If you hesitate, you wipe out!

"You're very wise," I said, shaking my head in wonder. "Very wise."

Dottie grabbed the handrail of the library steps and slowly worked her way up towards the door. I offered her my hand, but she shooed it away impatiently. "We need to find out for sure what Gaillard's relationship is to Marie. I'll play the bad cop. No offense, but you just don't have it in you."

When we entered the library, Gaillard looked up from a fashion magazine.

"Well, now, what do we have here?" he said in a bored voice. "This should be interesting."

He licked a finger and flipped the page in his magazine.

Dottie didn't waste any time putting him in his place. She grabbed the magazine and dropped it into the garbage can next to his desk. "Stop flapping your jaws. We're in the catbird seat now, buster."

If Gaillard was surprised, he didn't show it. He took a deep breath and quietly rearranged the items on his desk, as if it were a habit that helped him collect his thoughts. Then he smiled weakly and met Dottie's intense stare.

"I think I know what you're here for. If you're planning to interrogate me about Guy's murder or stolen antiquities, you can forget it. I don't know anything, and as you can see, I'm very busy."

Dottie pounded his desk with her fist. "Cut the chin music, Gaillard. Paul saw you and your little kewpie doll out on a heavy date."

She squinted her eyes and leaned in to watch his reaction, while I tried not to laugh.

"What a silly thought," Gaillard said. "Marie is my boss. That dinner was work related."

"Hogwash!" Dottie said.

She pulled the power cord out of the back of his computer and the monitor winked off.

Gaillard groaned and reached behind his computer to plug it back in. After fumbling around for a while, he finally gave up and crossed his arms, looking mildly annoyed. "It's absolutely none of your beeswax, but there's nothing going on between us. In case you hadn't noticed, Marie is twice my age. It's biologically impossible for me to have any attraction for her what-so-ever."

"That's the most cockamamie thing we've ever heard," Dottie said. She looked up at me with her magnified eyeballs and nudged me in the ribs. "Right, Paul?"

I opened my mouth to reply, but by now Dottie had gotten herself all wound up. All I could do was hang on and ride the wave.

"Hooey!" she cried. She grabbed the can of pencils on his desk and dumped them on the floor. Gaillard sighed and bent down to pick them up, and I crouched down to give him a hand.

I could see we weren't getting anywhere, so I took Dottie by the arm and ushered her out of the library, grinning sheepishly at Gaillard on the way out.

Once we were outside, I turned to Dottie. "That was rude. Gaillard may have been lying about his relationship with Marie, but he might have just been trying to protect her reputation. She's technically still a married woman, remember. Besides, I don't want to make any more enemies."

"Oh, stop being such a picklepuss." She pulled a phone from her pocket and started tapping the screen. "I managed to swipe his phone, didn't I?"

I couldn't help but be impressed. "Good work! Usually I wouldn't feel right going through someone's phone, but there's too much at stake here. Hurry up, so I can put it back before he finds it missing!"

"Bingo!" Dottie said, hunching over Gaillard's phone. "He's been texting Marie all morning, or rather, he's been texting *Sweet Pea* all morning."

I kept an anxious eye on the library doors, shielding Dottie and the phone with my body in case Gaillard appeared. "Is there any mention of Guy or the tapestry?"

Dottie shook her head while she swiped her finger over the screen. "I'm afraid not. Just more of the same mushy stuff." She turned off the phone and handed it to me. "Better get this back to him."

I ran back into the library and saw Gaillard searching his work area. There was no way I could return the phone without his noticing, so I just set it down in front of him. "This is for your lost and found. I found it on the lawn."

He looked at me angrily. "You know perfectly well that's my phone. That little goblin of yours took it."

There was no point in denying it, or confirming it either. All I could do was apologize. "Sorry for Dottie's behavior earlier. Guy was a very old friend of hers, and we're both frustrated by the police investigation. She reads way too many detective novels."

Gaillard pocketed the phone and his demeanor softened a little. "Alright, Paul. I won't hold it against you personally. But if she went through my phone and starts shooting her mouth off about anything she read, there might be another murder for you to solve."

Chapter 20

Dottie's apartment was just around the corner, facing a park where kids were swinging and climbing on playground equipment.

As soon as she showed me into her apartment, the sound of sizzling food and a delicious aroma hit me. I could hear water running in the kitchen.

"Make yourself at home," Dottie said, gesturing at the table.

In the middle of the table, I saw what appeared to be an electric barbecue. Meat, green peppers and onions were sizzling on the grill. I felt my mouth water. Beneath the cooking surface, there were small triangular pans with long handles. Curious, I slid one of the pans out then pushed it back in.

Dottie was delighted by the table setting. "My granddaughter must have wanted to surprise me. It appears we're having a traditional French Raclette. What luck! Those little pans you're playing with are for the individual servings. You grill the food on the top grill, put it in one of those pans, and cover the food with cheese. Then the pan goes back under the grill until the cheese melts. Voila."

The sound of running water stopped, and a girl wearing pink pajamas with a big white unicorn on them entered the room. She carried plates laden with fingerling potatoes, eggs, assorted meats, and vegetables. When she saw me, her eyes popped open in surprise. She set the plates down and ran out of the room.

I was dumbstruck. I looked back and forth from the swinging kitchen door to Dottie's grinning face. "Oh dear, didn't I mention it?" Dottie said innocently. "Sophie is my grand-daughter."

"I just assumed your granddaughter was a little girl."

"She will always be a little girl to me."

I remembered the silly package of tattoos in my hand, and looked around for a place to stash it. The package was too big to fit in my pants pocket, and I wasn't wearing a jacket. Could I stuff it in my pants?

Sophie came back in wearing jeans and a Crème de la Crêpe t-shirt and took a seat next to me. She sat stiffly in her chair, with her feet together and her hands on her knees.

"Hi, Sophie!" I said brightly. "This is a nice surprise. I had no idea you lived here."

She smiled back at me, her cheeks red. "I'm so embarrassed."

"Don't be. I thought your pajamas were cute. I've got the same ones."

She laughed, and the mood in the room became more comfortable.

Dottie appeared to be enjoying this. She smiled mischievously. "Paul has something for you, Sophie."

Sophie turned to me, her face beaming. "You have something for me?" She poked me as though she were trying to get candy from a piñata.

Why did everyone want to poke my stomach lately? Was I getting pudgy?

I reluctantly passed her the bag that I was hiding behind my back.

She smiled and tore into it. When she saw the tattoos, she acted like they were the greatest thing she'd ever received. Then she leaned over and gave me a friendly peck on the cheek.

I suddenly felt very warm. I looked over at Dottie,

who just smiled.

"I'm glad you like it. It was either that or a sack of wax lips," I said with an awkward smile. "I hope I'm not making extra work for you by being here?"

"Don't be silly," she said, pushing the sizzling food around the grill with a fork. "It's best to have friends over; raclette is a sociable meal and there are always leftovers."

"I'm lucky to have friends like you guys," I said.

Sophie removed one of the pans and started to fill it with pieces of cooked chicken, green peppers and potatoes. She gave me a sidelong glance. "I'm sure you've made lots of friends since you've been here."

Did she mean Francine? Perhaps she saw us together the other day after all.

"I've certainly met a lot of interesting people," I said vaguely. "It's been a crazy week."

I filled my pan as Sophie had done, and layered strips of cheese on top. Then I slid it into the grill and watched the cheese slowly bubble and melt. When I couldn't wait any longer, I took a bite and the world faded away.

"This is my new favorite food," I said, and meant it. I shoveled it all in my mouth and it was gone in seconds.

While I considered my next serving, I looked over at Sophie, who was already hard at work on her own. She put thin potato slices on a layer of partly melted cheese, then followed it with strips of filet mignon and more cheese. She then sprinkled cumin and basil over the top and put it into the grill to melt.

She caught my glance and smiled. "I'm making this one for you."

"Cool! Shall I make one for you?"

She eyed me with suspicion. "I guess so. You're not just going to put some cheese on a pickle are you?"

I spread my hands. "Would I do that? Don't worry, I'll make you a raclette fit for a queen."

Sophie giggled and gave me her empty pan.

"Now, where are the grapes?" I asked.

"Yuck! I change my mind."

"Just kidding," I said, artfully arranging an enormous pile of ingredients into her tray. "I'm going to try my best. I owe you for all those great crêpes you made me."

I turned to Dottie and said, "If you like what you see, I can make you one too. This is fun!"

"Thanks, but no thanks. Preparing them is half the fun." She was already sliding her second serving into the grill.

When I melted Sophie's raclette and showed her the result, she gave me a thumbs up and dug in. She nodded approvingly while she chewed.

Dottie said, "Sophie usually eats like a bird. You can come over any time and help me fatten her up."

"Glad to be of service," I said as I polished off my own plate.

It wasn't long before all the ingredients were gone and everyone was stuffed.

Sophie left the room and returned with a computer memory stick. "Here are the photos that I picked out for your guest rooms, Paul. I picked out the most contrasty ones that will look best in black and white. Thanks a bunch for the opportunity; it was very nice of you."

Dottie said, "Sophie has been working all night on those. You have my gratitude too, Paul."

I held up my hand in protest. "Just a minute. I'm not doing her any favors here; remember, I have a degree in fine art, and I know great photographs when I see them. This is a good deal for both of us. I'm getting free art for my walls, and hopefully making a few bucks, too."

Sophie looked at me as if she'd caught her cat

playing the piano. "You have an *art degree?*"

"I also have a business diploma from a community college. My dad made me take it in exchange for wasting four years in art school.. as he put it."

"That's amazing! Well, thanks again. No matter what you say, I appreciate it." She looked at her watch. "Gotta run. Bye, Paul. Bye, Grandma."

We said our good-byes, and I helped Dottie clear the table while we waited for our coffee to brew. Dottie was using an old-fashioned percolator, and soon an aroma of strong Turkish coffee filled the room.

When we sat down with our coffees, Dottie sighed. "Quite the little monkey, isn't she?"

"She sure is," I agreed, taking a sip. "Quite a monkey."

"Very smart too. She's learning Japanese right now."

"No, she isn't."

"Oh, yes. She loves to learn languages, but she's too shy to practice with real people. She's also a Chess Master—well, she would correct me and say the official title is *Candidate Master*."

"No, she isn't."

"Yes, she is! She's been competing for years. Her father is a Master; his rating is 200 points higher. I taught him when he was a boy, but he could beat me by the time he was ten."

Even though I was fascinated by Dottie's tall tales, I didn't feel comfortable talking about Sophie when she wasn't around. It was time to change the channel. "I've been thinking; I think it's time we got proactive in our investigation."

Dottie looked interested. "Oh, goody, we're on the case again. Where do we start?"

I nursed my coffee, holding it with both hands. "I was thinking about that. There's a good chance that the tapestry is the key to all of this. And since there was a murder, I'm betting that some money has changed hands."

"Always follow the money," Dottie agreed.

"If we could only see Guy's bank statements, I bet we would find a clue."

"Now you're on the trolley!" Dottie said. She set down her mug and went to her computer, a sleek expensive-looking model with an enormous screen.

I trailed behind her in disbelief. "You have access to his bank statements?"

"I told you earlier that I did his taxes."

"I assumed you just used the files in his office."

Dottie squinted. "Files? What decade are you living in?" Her bony fingers flew across the keyboard as she opened a browser and accessed a bank website. "I convinced Guy to buy me this spanking new computer to do his taxes, then I gave my old computer to Sophie." She turned to me and winked.

Dottie's expression changed. "That's odd. Guy must have changed his password."

My heart sank.

Dottie made a few unsuccessful attempts to guess the password, then stopped. "I only have one more attempt until we're locked out."

I searched my memory, and an idea came to me. "Try *born to pick* with no spaces."

Dottie carefully typed in it, then threw up her hands and whooped with joy. "Attaboy, Paul! It worked! How did you know?"

"That's what the T-shirt said that he died in."

"Oh," she said quietly. "Way to turn the mood around."

Guy's personal bank history appeared on the screen. Dottie scrolled through the records, looking through the lower half of her bifocals. She made sounds that alternated between curiosity and disapproval as she read. When she made a clucking sound with her tongue, I couldn't stand it any longer.

"What is it?" I cried out.

"Nothing, I just have some food in my dentures," she said absently.

Then she sat up straight. "Hello, what's this? There are huge money transfers to a company called BitSecure. What in heavens is that?"

"It's a Bitcoin exchange," I said.

Dottie just stared at me. I might as well have been speaking Inuktitut.

"Bitcoin is a type of electronic currency. It's used by criminals online because it's anonymous. You can use it to gamble, buy weapons, or buy drugs, and nobody including the government can trace it."

Dottie still looked confused. "How is this different from normal money? It's all electronic these days."

"The difference," I explained, "is that the money in your bank account and credit cards have no inherent value; they're just a reflection of cash that somebody else is holding for you. Bitcoins, on the other hand, are like gold coins. They have intrinsic value. If your computer is stolen and your Bitcoins are stored on it, then they're gone for good."

Dottie shook her head. "Will wonders never cease. So does this mean we have proof Guy was a criminal?"

"Not necessarily. Even though Bitcoins are often used in shady deals, they're also becoming mainstream. Back in Vancouver, there are Bitcoin vending machines popping up everywhere."

Dottie said, "But in this case, considering both the amount and the circumstances, it looks like Guy was up to his eyeballs in *some* type of mischief."

"Well, let's see what else we can find."

"Bingo!" Dottie exclaimed. "Here's one of the transfers to his ex-wife or separated wife, Marie. Until recently, she got the same amount every month. But this month, she didn't get anything."

I looked at the amount and whistled. "I can understand her getting upset. This amount gives her a pretty cushy life. I guess Guy must have found out about her affair with Gaillard."

Dottie said, "It doesn't seem like enough of a reason to bump someone off, although it could have been if they fought and she lost control."

"Print out the transactions. I think we need to figure out how he spent his Bitcoins."

My cell phone rang. The caller ID said Crème de la Crêpe.

I answered on the first ring. "Moshi Moshi."

I heard a snort of laughter on the other end of the line. It was Sophie. "You're such an idiot. Anyway, there's something going on outside your building. You might want to get over here."

Chapter 21

Back at my building, we found Napoleon standing out front with Pascal who I'd met at the Pétanque game, along with another man I didn't recognize who was wearing overalls and a tool belt. Napoleon gesticulated wildly and pointed at different features of the building, while Pascal took notes on his clipboard.

When Napoleon noticed us, he crossed his arms and smiled. "Oh-oh, Paul, I have some bad news for you..." He winced as thought it pained him to deliver it. "It appears as though renovations have been done without authorization." Then he opened his eyes wide and covered his mouth with his hand, feigning shock.

I heaved a sigh, "What the hell are you talking about?"

"It means you're in a lot of trouble. Perhaps you want to call your daddy now?"

I ignored him and turned to Pascal. "What's this all about?"

Pascal looked apologetic. "Unfortunately, Napoleon may be right about the trouble. He called me to report some building code violations, and I'm obliged to follow up on them."

I glared at Napoleon. I wasn't going to let my temper get the better of me. It had gotten me into trouble a few years back when some barney had snaked my waves once too often. I took my psychologist's advice and went to my happy place, slicing an epic wave in crystal clear water.

"Just lay it on me," I said to Pascal. "I'll deal with

it."

"Well, for starters, work was done on your windows without authorization."

"You mean a building permit?"

"Actually, I was referring to authorization from the city. Any time you make repairs that involve the exterior appearance of these old buildings, you need permission. But now that you mention it, there was no construction permit issued, either."

What a week this was shaping up to be!

"So there was no permit or permission," I said. "You realize that Napoleon is probably the one who made these renovations?"

"Be that as it may, it's up to the building owner to secure the permits," Pascal said. "I really am sorry to give you this news."

"It's not your fault," I said, glaring at Napoleon. "So how do I fix this?"

"Well, there's something else. It's about your store."

I sighed loudly. "What about my store?"

"The layout of your main floor was changed to accommodate it."

"No permission?" I asked.

"No permission."

"Is there anything else?"

"Just some minor things; I'll get you a list. Nothing urgent though."

That was something, I guess. Napoleon, standing within earshot, was overjoyed by the conversation. I'd never seen him smile before.

"So what happens now? I pay a fine?"

"At the very least, yes. But in cases like this, I've seen court orders issued for you to return the building to its original condition at your own expense."

The news hit me like a ton of bricks. A major renovation like that would cost a fortune, money that I didn't have. I'd be buried in construction projects and red tape until Christmas. My dream was turning into a nightmare.

He saw my dismay. "Don't panic yet. That's the worst case scenario. The good news is that the work was done well, and the windows were restored to match the original design. These rules were put in place to prevent people from ruining our heritage buildings with ridiculous changes like vinyl windows. So I think there will just be a small fine for the exterior issues."

I exhaled, relieved.

Pascal added, "I'll have to discuss the interior with my superiors. I can't promise anything, but I hope that we can overlook it because the work was done years ago. And once again, the contractor did a good job."

"It was a perfect job! I did it." Napoleon snapped.

His mood had started to go downhill again when he saw his plan to ruin me hadn't worked. He turned and headed back to the antique store. Clearly he'd lost interest in his scheme, and I was left to pick up the pieces.

Pascal climbed back into his truck with his assistant, and leaned out the window. "Try not to worry too much. I'll do what I can for you."

Dottie and I watched Napoleon lumber down the street and disappear into his antique store.

"The police tape is gone," I said to her. "The police must have everything they need from the crime scene. I really wish we could take a look around too."

Dottie turned to me. "Do you think the police might have missed something? They're the experts; I'm sure they know what they're doing."

"That's assuming they know what they're looking for. They don't know anything about the tapestry, for starters. And I'd like to have a look at Guy's computer. I'm sure the police have been though it for obvious stuff, but I'd like to see if there's any mention of the tapestry in his emails."

"Why don't we go tonight when it gets dark?" Dottie suggested.

"Actually, that idea crossed my mind too. But there's no reason for both of us to get into trouble. Breaking and entering is a serious crime." *I should know.*

For just a moment, she looked deflated, but then her expression became shrewd. "Mark my words, young man. There's no way on God's green earth I'm missing out on this spicy caper. I know Guy's business *and* his filing system. You need me there."

I looked down at her, unsure what to do. She looked so eager, but Sophie would never forgive me if I got her grandmother arrested. But maybe if we got caught together, it wouldn't look as nefarious. After all, if I were committing a crime, why would I bring along a witness? Also, she could be right about coming in handy. I wanted to get in and out as quickly as possible.

"Okay I surrender," I said, throwing up my hands. "It's against my better judgment, but you can come. Remember though, we have to move quickly and quietly. I'm afraid you might not be able to keep up."

"Oh, baloney! I'm spry as a fifty year old. Can I wear my black leotard?"

I didn't need long to think about that one. "No."

"Face paint?"

"Um, no."

She sighed. "What kind of caper is this, Paul? Can we bring flashlights, at least?"

"It's not a caper! But, yes, we will bring flashlights."

"Ooh! I've always wanted to sneak around an office with a flashlight. It's so exciting!"

"Try to contain yourself; we have all afternoon before we leave. Do you have enough to keep you busy until then?"

"Are you kidding? I still have the Celine and Richard figures to make. I think we have everything we need for the Celine figure, but we should make a new armature. The male frames are all the wrong size, and definitely the wrong shape."

"Sounds good. And I'm going to start something I should have done as soon as I arrived. I'm going to give those guest rooms upstairs a top to bottom cleaning. I may not have the best amenities in town, but I can certainly build my reputation on being the cleanest, with a great location."

Dottie edged away. "Don't ask me to help; the upstairs is all yours. My responsibilities are limited to the gift shop and museum."

I could hardly complain about her creating her own job description. After all, I wasn't paying her anything. I knew someday I'd have to hire someone to handle the cleaning and reservations when the rental business picked up, but for now, I wanted to learn every part of the business inside and out—and keep my meager income stream for myself.

I smiled at Dottie. "Agreed! And I appreciate everything you do. Don't worry, I actually like to clean. It's good mindless work."

Dottie poured herself a coffee and headed downstairs. In no time at all, I heard her sewing machine start up.

Before going upstairs with Beachley to look for cleaning supplies, I suddenly remembered that I hadn't called my absentee guests. I'd been so distracted by the museum and the tapestry that I'd neglected the most important thing of all: the rentals. There wasn't much time left before the summer festival, so I had to do everything I possibly could to turn around my tenuous situation.

I sat down next to the reservation book, took a deep breath, and dialed the first reservation on the list. The booking was for two full months in my best room. I was anxious to ask why they'd canceled without the simple courtesy of calling. I could potentially lose weeks of revenue while I found a replacement guest.

The lady who answered the phone sounded friendly at first, but her mood changed completely when I introduced myself. "Oh, it's you. I've been trying to reach you for days! If I don't get my deposit back immediately you'll be hearing from my lawyer. That's a promise."

I was so puzzled that it took me a moment to formulate my response. "We expected you here a few days ago. I was just calling to find out if you were still coming."

It was the lady's turn to hesitate. When she spoke again, her voice sounded more confused than angry. "You said your name is Paul, right? I got an email from you cancelling my reservation. You said you'd gone bankrupt."

"It wasn't from me," I said, my mind reeling. "I just took over the building. Someone must be playing a very bad joke on one of us."

"Some joke! Our vacation was ruined. There isn't another room in the whole city until after the festival!"

"I'm very sorry," I said. "I'll do everything I can to fix this. But first, what email address was the message sent from?"

She checked, and spelled it out for me.

Napoleon!

I couldn't believe what was happening. Napoleon must have contacted everyone in my reservation book, and probably ruined any slim chance I had of turning a profit within my three-month deadline. My future was circling the bowl, so I had to roll up my sleeves and grab what I could before it went down the drain forever.

I was tempted to give her Napoleon's contact details so she could blast him herself, but I knew that would be unprofessional. Right now it was more important to make her a happy customer again.

"That was the previous owner," I said. "Maybe he didn't realize I'd be continuing the rental business. At any rate, here's what I propose. I still have your room available if you want it. The previous owner didn't pass along your deposit, but that's not your problem. I'll even make one of your weeks free of charge."

When she hesitated, I continued, "You'll absolutely love the room, and the location can't be beat. I'll do everything I can to make your stay perfect. I'd like to have you as my regular guest in the future."

"Okay," she said finally. "We'll be there this weekend."

After I ended the call, I sat in silence for a moment, imagining what I'd like to do to Napoleon. Truth be told, punching noses isn't nearly as satisfying as one might think—most pleasures are greatest in anticipation.

But right now, I had more calls to make.

Each guest in the reservation book had a similar story. A hefty deposit was paid, then Napoleon, posing as me, cancelled their reservation. All of them were understandably frantic about their deposits, which were as high as fifty percent of the total bill.

I managed to get many of them to keep their reservation by offering some free days. Unfortunately, some insisted on a refund of their deposit, which I didn't have. In every case, I apologized and made arrangements to reimburse them with my own money.

When I'd finished my calls, I made some calculations.

Taking into consideration the free weeks I'd offered,

plus the lost deposit revenue, not to mention the money I was refunding from my own pocket, I wouldn't actually turn a profit from their rentals. But the good news is that I wouldn't lose money, either. If I simply refunded all the deposits, I wouldn't have a penny left to my name.

I really needed a distraction at that point, and cleaning the guest rooms was the best way to clear my mind.

I found a large supply closet at the end of a hall that housed a shabby washer and dryer, as well as cleaners, brushes, and a very reliable, very upright-looking Electrolux vacuum.

I moved from room to room, cleaning every nook and cranny, including the parts that nobody notices such as the undersides of tables, the tops of light fixtures and the backs of toilets. I carried a pen and paper with me, making a shopping list as I went along. Like the wax museum, I wanted to do a mini-makeover of every room, until I had the chance to renovate them properly. For now, that just meant new shower faucets and toilet seats, and maybe some fresh linens and bedspreads.

Just as I was finishing up and switching off the vacuum cleaner, I noticed Dottie standing next to me.

"Giddy up, Paul! It's time to get moving!"

Chapter 22

Against my explicit advice, Dottie was dressed in black pants and a black turtleneck, and her face was covered in black paint.

"Where did you find that outfit?" I asked.

"You'd be surprised by what we have in the scrap material bin."

"How'd you plan to cross the street without someone noticing? They'll think you're crazy."

"It's dark out. I'll be invisible."

"Alright," I conceded. "Walk quickly but look natural. Don't bring any attention to us."

By a miracle we made our way to the back alley of Tremblay Antiques without being spotted. I noticed the same parked cars were there that had been there since the morning of Guy's murder. Judging by the rust, they may not have budged in years. I suspected they belonged to tenants since all the windows facing the alley had small air conditioners and curtains, and appeared to be apartments.

The back door of Tremblay's was lit up by a security light mounted above it. We huddled close to the door, trying to keep our faces from being seen by anyone who might be peeking out of their second floor windows.

Dottie's idea of wearing dark makeup might have been a good one, after all.

She punched a number into the keypad but the knob wouldn't turn. "I guess the code was changed."

"I'm surprised Napoleon is so quick to change the door code," I said. "He seems to use the same password for everything else. In my opinion, that's a much bigger security risk."

I wasn't ready to give up. I had some experience breaking into buildings—not as a thief, but because I used to get a kick out of sneaking into abandoned houses and factories. Even though the back wall of the store had no windows, there was a fire escape on the second story. A steel ladder hung down from it and stopped a few feet above our heads.

I pulled Dottie away from the bright security light and into the shadows next to the building. "Does anyone live on the second floor?"

"No, Guy used it for storage. Every inch of this building is packed with stuff. Why?"

"I might be able to get in through the fire escape on the second floor. Just wait here and don't make a sound. If I get in, I'll open the back door for you."

Dottie nodded and pretended to button her lips.

I found an old bicycle frame and leaned it against the wall under the fire-escape, using it to extend my reach to the lowest rung of the fire ladder. I climbed up to the platform without much trouble. Luckily, it was directly above the security light. If anyone happened to look my way, their eyes would be so blinded by the light that everything else, including us, would be dark.

I crouched on the platform next to the large window that doubled as an emergency exit.

Unlike the heavy shuttered windows on the front of these old buildings, this window was a cheap vinyl design with two sliding panes. I forced it open without much trouble; the only resistance came from years of grime and rotting wood.

I switched on my flashlight and climbed into the darkness.

Dottie was right; the place was crammed with artifacts, boxes, and shipping crates. They were mostly large items like stained glass panels, heavy furniture, and scrap iron. It reminded me of the abandoned buildings I used to explore, except, on this occasion, I was completely sober, and my senses were sharpened by adrenaline.

The room was so large that my flashlight only illuminated the objects closest to me. Everything else was swallowed in blackness. I stayed close to the walls as I moved through the shadows, until I found a wide stairway leading down to the main level. I passed through a bead curtain at the bottom of the stairs, and found myself back in familiar territory again at the back of Tremblay Antiques.

Napoleon had neglected to arm the security system, so I didn't worry about setting off an alarm as I cracked open the rear door and whistled for Dottie.

"Here I am," a voice in the darkness whispered. She slipped through the door and I quietly closed it behind her. "My heart is beating like crazy! Wow, it's dark in here, isn't it?"

The beam from my flashlight was growing orangey and dim. "Dang, I forgot to put fresh batteries in it. Now what?"

Dottie reached into her pocket and pulled out a smart phone. "No problem; I downloaded a flashlight app!"

Dottie owned a smart phone? I put out my hand like a crossing guard. If I'd had a whistle, I would have blown it. "Wait a minute; just hold the phone. Pun intended. A few days ago, you were ranting about smart phones and technology. And now you're downloading apps?"

She looked at me incredulously. "I said I didn't *like* phones; I never said I didn't *own* one."

Surprisingly, her phone put out more lumens than my dying flashlight.

"Well, it does makes a decent flashlight," I said with

a smile. "A $600 flashlight."

Dottie said, "It's much more than a flashlight. I can also use it to see what Sophie's up to on the Facebook and the Tumblr."

"You don't have to say *the*. It's just *Facebook*," I said.

"No, I'm pretty sure she uses both of them."

"You mean she uses both of the services, not both of the words."

Dottie looked me and shook her head. "I don't know how a man your age can be so confused by technology. I'll explain it to you later. My phone is going to run out of juice if we don't hurry."

We made our way to Guy's office and I switched on his computer. The room was soon filled with the pale glow of his screen.

"We won't need the light from your phone any more."

She switched it off, and we sat down in front of the computer.

"Let's check out his inventory records first," I said. "If the tapestry was ever in Guy's possession, it might be catalogued."

I accessed Guy's business software, searching for every possible keyword relating to Gobelin tapestries, but no results came up.

"Can we search by date?" Dottie asked.

"Great idea!" I selected a two-week range leading up to Guy's death. Dozens of items appeared, but still no tapestry. "Nope. Nothing."

Dottie took a folded-up paper from her pocket and smoothed it out on the desk. "I made a print-out of the anonymous Bitcoin transactions; let's see if we can match some of them up."

I was impressed. She acted loopy sometimes, but when it came right down to it, Dottie was as sharp as a tack. "What would I do without you?"

Dottie beamed at the compliment, then put on her glasses and leaned forward to study the screen. "Boy, oh boy! We're on to something. For every one of the large money transfers, he added something to his inventory within an hour or two."

"So this proves he *was* buying suspicious artifacts with Bitcoin. Most likely illegally. But we still have no direct connection between Guy and the tapestry. I wish we could see his communications with the seller. Maybe he had an appointment to buy the tapestry, but something went wrong?"

"Hmm. Maybe there's something in his emails?" Dotty suggested.

"It's worth checking," I agreed. "I know that if I were making shady deals, I'd avoid using a phone. Who knows what government agencies are listening, or what sorts of phone records are being kept? I'd want to stay as anonymous as possible by using chat rooms or email."

I checked through all of his recent emails, including his deleted folder, but found nothing suspicious.

"Chances are the police have been through this already," I said with a heavy sigh. "But let's see what I can find in his browsing history."

Dottie waited while I checked the internet browser on Guy's computer. "Rats. No history. He had it set to delete his history every time he shut down." I paused to think. "I have one more idea. Guy wanted to be anonymous since he was using an anonymous payment method. So it stands to reason that he'd want to use an anonymous email account too. He might have used one of those free email services. If he did, there will probably be clues in his cookies."

"So now you're a cookie expert. No surprise there," Dottie quipped.

"No, a cookie is a piece of information that some websites leave on your computer to store information about you."

"I know what cookies are, Paul," she snapped. "I wasn't born yesterday, you know."

You can say that again.

I searched through Guy's cookies. "Here we go; he has an email account at a site called GhostMail. According to his cookies, his username is...um...never mind."

"What is it?" Dottie prompted.

I winced and pointed at the screen.

Dottie leaned in for a look. "Ooh, he was a live wire, that one!" Dottie said.

I shuddered. "Anyway, let's check it out."

I called up the GhostMail site and it logged me in automatically. "We're in! The messages don't go very far back; I guess he was careful to delete them. But we still have his messages for the past few weeks."

I noticed that a day or two prior to each of the big purchases, there was a paragraph describing the item being sold. Guy would reply with a dollar amount followed by a time, along with the word *fountain* or *cannon*.

"I think we found what we're looking for," I said, grinning. "I guess *fountain* and *canon* are the exchange locations. And look here! The last message is about the tapestry. It was written on Monday, the day before Guy was murdered."

Dottie whistled. "Guy was going to pay 150 grand for it. That's a lot of money."

"But only a fraction of what it's worth. Marie explained to me that selling the artifact is the hard part. The person who does the stealing only gets a small part of the item's value. Anyway, it looks like they planned to meet at a fountain somewhere. Five hours past their scheduled rendezvous, Guy got a message asking where the money was, but he didn't reply."

"Do you think Guy double-crossed him?" Dottie asked.

I scratched my head. "Why would he? You saw those Bitcoin transactions; he buys expensive things like this all the time. It's not that much money for him, really. And how could he double-cross him? Either they both show up at the rendezvous point to make the exchange, or they don't."

"Maybe it was an anonymous exchange, like kidnappers do to collect a ransom. The seller hides the tapestry in the bushes around the fountain. Guy shows up later, maybe wears a disguise, and retrieves it. When he gets back here, he transfers the cash, takes a picture of his artifact and adds it to his inventory."

I made a face that said her theory was plausible. "So on Monday, the seller probably believed he'd been cheated when no money came through, and stopped by to confront and kill Guy before the shop opened."

Just then, there was a faint clicking sound. Someone was unlocking the front door of the store.

Dottie and I froze and looked at each other with wide eyes. Old buildings always made strange sounds, so I desperately hoped it was nothing. But a moment later when the bell over the front door tinkled, my worst fears were confirmed.

I switched off the computer and crept to the office door. I expected the store lights to turn on, but it remained dark—so dark, in fact, that I could barely see my hand in front of my face. If it were just me, I'd have gone out the back and ran like hell. But there was no way Dottie could keep up.

"Dottie," I whispered. "Come here, and don't make a sound."

When I felt her standing next to me, I grabbed her

arm and led her toward the place where I'd remembered seeing a storage closet. I felt along the wall until I found the door frame and ushered her inside. I squeezed in after her and pulled the door closed.

Dottie whispered, "Are you using this as an excuse to get fresh?"

"Yes, Dottie. That's exactly what I'm doing." I rolled my eyes, even though she couldn't see them.

It was a strange time to be taking stock of my life, but at that moment it's what I found myself doing. Just a few weeks ago I'd been surfing in Vancouver at Long Beach without a care in the world, never knowing that in a few weeks I'd be embroiled in a double homicide, and playing seven minutes in heaven with an centenarian.

"Will you stop breathing? It frightens me," she said.

"Shh!"

Dottie gasped. "Oh! I feel bones!"

"That's me. Let go."

There must be duct tape in here somewhere, I thought.

Guy had a lot of inventory in his store, so Dottie's voice probably wouldn't carry beyond the office. Or at least, I hoped it wouldn't.

When we heard footsteps just outside of the office, we both got real quiet, real fast.

Every nerve of my body was on fire. I was prepared to fight for our lives if someone opened the closet. As long as no guns were involved, I stood a pretty good chance. I'd been in more than my share of fights in the past. Surfers may be known for being easy-going, but they can get downright nasty if you drop in on their wave.

I pushed the door open a few inches and peered through the crack.

A dark figure entered and moved slowly through the

office, sweeping a powerful flashlight around the room. When the light passed over the closet where we were hiding, it hit me dead in the eyes and momentarily blinded me. Then the light moved again.

Dottie gripped my arm with a vice-like grip. She was certainly getting the excitement she was looking for.

The chair creaked as the stranger took a seat in front of Guy's computer. A moment later, the screen came on and illuminated the strangers face.

I couldn't believe my eyes.

It was Marie!

Dottie and I waited as still as wax figures while Marie poked away on Guy's keyboard. For several minutes, she typed, sighed, and drummed her fingers on the desk. Finally, she switched off Guy's computer and began rifling through his file cabinet, one drawer at a time.

My legs started to cramp and my arm tingled. Dottie's death grip on my arm was cutting off my circulation. I wasn't sure how much longer I could wait. I was, however, very pleased by how quiet Dottie was.

After a few more minutes, Marie slammed the file drawer shut and marched out of the room. I waited until I heard her leave through the front door, then I put my hand on one of the closet shelves to straighten myself up. All at once, they crashed to the floor and made an enormous racket.

We stumbled out of the closet, tripping over office supplies and laughing with relief.

"Did you see who it was?" Dottie asked.

"You're not going to believe this. It was Marie from the Settlement Museum."

"Marie! Are you sure?"

"Absolutely. She was looking for something, but whatever it was, I don't think she found it. She seemed frustrated when she left."

"She was wasting her time searching Guy's files," Dottie said. "Guy was always behind in his paperwork—it drove me crazy at tax time." She pointed to a cardboard file box next to his desk. "That box probably contains a few months' worth of things waiting to be filed. It's his in-basket, he just threw everything on top of the pile."

I snatched the file box and headed for the back door. "Let's bounce! We can sort through this tomorrow."

After seeing Dottie home, I brought the file box up to my room and went through the papers. Nothing appeared interesting—mostly receipts, purchase orders and signed agreements.

I was exhausted and decided to call it an early night. Tomorrow I'd pay Marie a visit at the museum and ask her some hard questions.

Beachley jumped into bed and curled up next to me with a tired grunt. I turned off the bedside light and watched the moon through my window.

From somewhere very far away, I heard accordion music.

Was Marie searching for evidence that linked her to the crimes? Or maybe Guy was blackmailing her, and now that he was dead, she wanted to retrieve whatever it was he was holding against her? Or maybe she was searching for a will?

I needed answers, fast. Who knew when another murder might occur, and who the next victim might be?

What if the next break-in was at Dottie and Sophie's apartment?

Chapter 23

When I arrived at the Settlement Museum the next morning, the security guard waved me right through. "Take the elevator to the basement. Ms. Tremblay is waiting for you there."

I felt strangely disappointed by the cheerfulness of the guard, and by Marie's willingness to see me. I had braced myself for a conflict and expected a lot more resistance.

Marie greeted me when I got off the elevator. "Hi, Paul; it's nice to see you again! I hope you don't mind if we do a walk and talk, I have a lot of work to do."

Her smile didn't look sincere. I could tell something was bothering her. After what had gone down the previous night, I could hardly be surprised.

"A walk and talk would be fine," I said. "Thanks for the tour of the dig site yesterday. I appreciate the backstage pass." I looked her straight in the eye to gauge her reaction to my words. "I was surprised to see Bernard there."

"Bernard Gaillard is one of my best workers in the field," she said innocently. "He has a lot of interest in the dig, and he's a very patient worker There's a lot of slow digging in the dirt, and sometimes you don't find anything at all. If you find larger items, like this canon we found, it can take weeks to dig it out."

As we walked, she gestured at a large cast iron canon that looked surprisingly good for something that had been buried for centuries.

"How do you go about excavating something that

large?" I asked.

She stopped next to the canon and rested her hand on it. "Usually, your shovel would strike the top of the item first. Then you slowly dig around the object, being careful to use as little force as possible. We do the excavation in layers, and use brushes to even out the ground at each level before taking a photograph. It's a long process because we want to record as much information as we can at each step. Believe it or not, we even label the changes in dirt color using a Munsell Soil Chart."

She grabbed a small brown ringed binder from a table.

"What kind of information can you get from that?" I asked.

"We need to record the soil color at each layer. Different colors can represent different time periods." She held up the book. "This allows us to accurately describe the color of both the dirt and of the artifacts we find. We can't just say something is brown or white, since there are a lot of possible shades, and everyone describes colors differently."

She flipped open the book at random. The page was covered by a rainbow grid of color swatches of different shades, similar to what you'd find at paint stores. Marie continued, "Each page represents a hue, which is the overall color itself. Moving left to right across the page we have changes in value, which is the lightness of the color. Then vertically on the page we have the chroma. That's the strength of the color."

She selected a fragment of pottery from a tray and flipped through the book. "After you find the page that best matches the color, you hold the item behind the page so that it appears through the little holes next to each color. When you find the perfect match—voila— you know the color's hue, chroma and value."

As much as I enjoyed getting the dirt on Munsell charts, I was anxious to ask Marie the million dollar question: Was it possible for someone to remove something from the ground, and then put it *back* in the dirt without anyone noticing? But there was a fair to high chance that I'd be asking the very person who'd stolen the tapestry and committed two murders.

To get the information I needed, I had to excavate the truth like an archaeologist, digging around the question rather than risk my life blurting it out.

We resumed our walk. "So what are these wooden drawers along the walls?" I asked.

"They're artifact drawers. Many of them contain items we've found at the dig site. They haven't all been catalogued yet. It's a big job and we are understaffed."

She pulled open one of the drawers and motioned for me to take a look. It looked like the junk drawer in our kitchen back home, except everything looked rusty, twisted and dirty.

I said, "Compared to all these little coins and pieces of pottery, it must have been exciting to find that chest."

She closed the drawer. "It was the highlight of my career. We're keeping it under wraps until the New France festival. We'll make an official announcement then."

Marie looked at me for a moment as though she had a really big secret, but wasn't sure if she should spill the beans. The temptation won out. She led me to a well-lit table in the middle of the room, and pulled back a tarp to reveal a wooden chest.

The solid wood trunk, which apparently was once richly varnished, was now faded and worn, creating the type of beautiful finish that interior decorators would give their eye teeth for. It was reinforced with iron straps and corners. The side handles were also made of iron, as well as the front clasp that once held a lock. On the table next to the chest, there were photos that had been taken every few hours, documenting it's discovery and excavation.

"It looks almost brand new," I said in wonder. "Even pressure-treated wood gets rotten after a decade in the ground."

Marie nodded. "It was well preserved because it wasn't in direct contact with the soil where moisture would have rotted it. That alcove you saw at the dig site was enclosed by stone on all sides, except for the front of the alcove where there were once hinged doors. The doors would have held back the soil when the fort was buried. Even though the doors eventually rotted away, the alcove itself remained hollow, and so the chest was perfectly preserved even after being buried underground for three centuries."

"So if the chest had been just sitting in an alcove, it must have been easy to excavate it?" I asked.

"You'd think so, but nothing in archaeology is easy. There was a small amount of dirt and a lot of loose stones around the chest. We didn't know how fragile the chest was, so we had to remove it slowly and carefully. The whole process took days. It was a real test of patience because we couldn't open the lid and peek inside until we had it all the way out."

I considered the implications. The thief could have removed the chest from the alcove, found the tapestry, and replaced the chest without anyone knowing. There wouldn't have been any of the tell-tale evidence you would have by removing something from packed dirt. The loose rubble in the alcove could easily have been replaced without anyone being the wiser.

Marie excused herself to help a colleague who'd suddenly appeared beside her, so I took the opportunity to examine the excavation photos.

190 Death of a Dummy

The time that each picture had been taken was recorded in the corner. I reasoned that if someone had disturbed the chest in the dig site, I should be able to figure out exactly when it happened.

I glanced at Marie to make sure she was still occupied, and positioned the Munsell soil book over the first photograph in the sequence. After I identified the soil color, I moved the book over the next photos in the sequence, looking carefully for any changes. Near the end of the sequence, I saw something that made my heart race.

The hue was completely different. In fact, I had to flip to a whole new page in the Munsell book to match the color.

I couldn't believe that nobody had noticed it before. The change had happened some time between the end of Bernard's shift, and a few hours into the next morning.

I had the information I needed, and quickly replaced the Munsell book on the table.

When Marie returned and prepared to show me the rest of the basement, I decided to cut our visit short and confronted her. I put my hand on her arm and lowered my voice. "I saw you going into Tremblay Antiques last night."

I decided it would be better to let her believe that I saw her entering the antique store from outside, rather than admit to my own illegal entry.

I felt her stiffen. For a moment, she didn't move or say a word, then she pulled me into a side room where we couldn't be heard. "I don't see how it's any of your business. I still have my old key to the store, you know."

There was no turning back now. "You didn't turn on any lights, and you were using a flashlight. Kind of strange, if you ask me."

Her eyes flashed. "Nobody asked you, Paul. That's the point."

Now I was the one who was getting irritated. "Whether you like it or not, I intend to find out what happened to Guy. You can either explain it all to me, or you can talk to the police. I think they might be interested to know about your romance with Gaillard too, *Sweet Pea*."

That seemed to take the wind out of her, and her expression softened. Suddenly, she looked very tired, and very old.

"Okay, here it is," Marie began. "Guy found out that Gaillard and I have been seeing each other. On the weekend before Guy died, he told me he stopped my alimony payments, and he bullied me into signing a divorce agreement. When I said I wanted to consult a lawyer first, he blackmailed me. He told me that if I didn't sign his papers, he'd tell my bosses that I was selling him antiquities from the museum."

"Were you?"

"Of course not! But then he showed me an item from the museum's collection. I don't know where he got it from, but it didn't matter. He could make a strong case against me. So I signed it."

She paused, and tears formed in her eyes. "When Guy was found dead, I realized he may have still had the divorce papers at the antique store, since there hadn't been time to deliver them to the courthouse. I couldn't bear the idea of losing an estate worth millions, and the thought of it going to that ass-hat Napoleon was even more unthinkable. He's the one who killed Guy! He inherits Tremblay Antiques, you know."

"So I've heard."

"Look, I know it looks bad for me. Landry already thinks I killed Guy, and if he knew that I had a strong motive, he'd arrest me. You have to believe me, I'd never do that to Guy. Even though things went downhill with us, we still had a lot of good years together."

"I'm not sure what I believe." I turned my back on her and walked back to the elevator.

I could still hear the sound of her sobbing as the elevator doors closed.

Across from the settlement museum, I passed by the large water fountain where Remy had performed his bronze statue act. It was the fanciest fountain in the city—the type you find in the town squares of European cities. A stone bench wrapped all the way around it, and water cascaded down from bronze sculptures depicting a historic Quebec scene.

I noticed that the smallest of the bronze statues looked out of place. It was positioned, by itself, at the very edge of the fountain with the figure's head resting in his hands. I stopped for a closer look and discovered it was my new friend Cliff.

"How's it going?" I asked with a smile as I approached him. "We met a few days ago."

"Yeah, I remember," Cliff drawled. "I'm fine. You hear about the accident?"

"You mean Remy? Yup, I saw the ambulances and police cars. But it was no accident. He was killed with a pick axe from the dig site."

Cliff winced. "Well, I ain't never!" He shook his head with wonder. "I tell you, there's no respect for us performers no more. I'm gonna get me a gun for protection."

"I don't know if that's such a good idea," I said.

It occurred to me that he might have some information about Remy. There was also a good chance that the police didn't even think to interview one of

Remy's fellow performers. "When's the last time you saw him?"

"I ain't seen hide nor hair of him since Tuesday. I knowed there must be something wrong, and I found out yesterday what befell him. So me being the entrepreneuring type, I figured he wouldn't mind if I borrowed his act at the fountain here. Lord knows I weren't making diddley squat as a stone statue."

"What about the day before that, on Monday? Did you see him then?"

Cliff scratched his chin, then inspected his fingernails to see if any bronze paint came off. "Yeah, I seen him Monday night, and it was most peculiar indeed."

I felt my excitement rise. "How so?"

"Well, I seen him doing his bronze dummy act here all afternoon clear through to night. Beats the heck out of me why he'd work so many hours."

I felt a pang of guilt. That was my first day in town when Remy had promised to earn enough money to pay his back rent.

Cliff continued, "I weren't watchin' him the whole time, but at some point he drug somethin' out of the shrubs that looked like a rolled-up carpet, and then he hid behind that there building and watched the shrubs."

It must have been the tapestry, I thought. I'd already figured out that an exchange was supposed to take place that night. And now I knew with absolute certainty that Remy was somehow involved.

"Think carefully," I said. "What happened next?"

"Well, a while later, a man with a cane came up and looked through the shrubs and got hisself mighty worked up, and left in a stink when he couldn't find what he was lookin' for. When he got up the road a piece, Remy followed him carrying that rug he found."

Suddenly, everything became clear.

I needed to compare notes with Dottie and come up with a plan.

But first, I needed to get home and have a closer look through Guy's file box.

Chapter 24

Considering everything that had gone missing lately, I was surprised Guy's file box was still under my bed. Then again, the only person who knew I had it was Dottie, and I'd crossed her off my list of suspects a long time ago.

Now that I knew what I was looking for, I found Marie's signed divorce agreement after only a few minutes of searching.

Marie was right. Guy hadn't had a chance to submit it to the courthouse, so on paper they were still legally married. She stood to inherit a fortune. I put the document back in the box until I could decide what to do with it.

When I went back down to the gift shop, I heard the faint sound of Dottie's sewing machine through the open basement door. There was also a strong scent of candles in the air coming from the direction of a stainless steel cart that I hadn't noticed before. I recognized it as the wax hand station that was being stored in the basement.

There were several stainless steel chambers of molten wax submerged in a temperature controlled water bath. Each chamber had a different shade of wax, and a larger chamber to one side contained clear water. There were also paper towels, hand lotion, and some curious looking utensils.

Just as I started to fiddle with the buttons and knobs, Dottie came up the stairs. "Not bad for an old lady, eh? I brought it up all by myself."

"Oh, man, it's awesome!" I said. "We can make some serious cash with this."

"You're darn tootin'!" Dottie said, smiling ear to ear. "We can charge eight bucks a pop."

I poked the tip of my finger into one of the wax chambers, and felt the wax tighten on my skin. "Is this how you made the hands for the Étienne exhibit?"

"Oh, heavens, no! These are only good for souvenirs. What you end up with is a smooth featureless hand that looks like a rubber glove."

"Hmm. Too bad we can't sell good quality hands," I said.

"Later, we could do some better ones, but we'd have to charge more. The process takes more time and manpower. We'd need to take a life cast with alginate, which picks up the actual skin texture including wrinkles, veins, and tiny hairs. Then you use the cast to make your hand, and it takes several hours for it to set."

"The ones in the museum are amazing," I said. "But for now, I'm sure tourists would be happy with these. How about a test run?"

"That was the idea. Roll up your sleeves and cover your hand and wrist in the lotion. Then keep your hand still, and dip it back and forth between one of the wax pots and the cold water."

I did as she instructed. I made a *hang loose* sign by closing all my fingers except for the thumb and pinky. The wax was hot, but not uncomfortably so. It felt pleasant, actually. I wondered if it could double as a spa treatment.

"Don't move your fingers, and feel free to fix the uneven parts between dips. If you don't, they'll just get worse."

"How many times do I do this?" I asked.

"For adults, it takes around ten dips. Five for kids."

I noticed my hand was getting thicker and heavier

with each dip. Just as Dottie said, there was zero detail. It was a bit disappointing, and I was anxious to try the life cast technique some time.

Dottie saw that my hand was ready, and used a metal implement to free the wax shell from my hand. Then she sealed off the base by dipping it back in the wax.

She handed me the finished product. I wasn't sure what I was supposed to do with it next. If I'd thought to put my fingers in a different configuration, I would have had a great one to send home to Todd.

"I think we have a winning product here!" I said. "Should we shut the equipment off now?"

"Already did. We can keep reheating the same wax so nothing is wasted."

I glanced at the clock. "It looks like we missed lunch. I'll whip up some coffee and snacks. I think I made some headway on our case, and I'd like to run some things by you."

I made the coffee and sliced up a chocolate cake while Dottie made herself comfortable in one of the wingback chairs near the fireplace. I was really looking forward to using the fireplace when winter came around. I was almost tempted to crank the air conditioning just so I could light it up. But for now, it was enough to sit near the hearth with a delicious dark roast coffee and enjoy the smell of last winter's ashes. I plunked our cakes and coffees down next to our chairs.

"So," I began, blowing on my coffee to cool it down. "I paid Marie another visit. She admitted to breaking into Guy's office. She was looking for the divorce papers he'd made her sign."

"That doesn't look too good for her, does it?"

"No, it doesn't. And I found the papers she was looking for in the file box I took home. I also found photo evidence that proves the chest was removed from the dirt at the dig site during the night and then replaced."

Dottie narrowed her eyes. "It sounds like you struck pay dirt." Realizing her pun, she smiled faintly. "But from the way you're telling it, I get the feeling you haven't told me the good part yet."

"As usual your instincts are bang on..."

I took a big bite of my cake and closed my eyes while I enjoyed it. Then I blew on my coffee some more and took a few little sips. It was my turn to keep Dottie in suspense. She'd done the same thing to me when she'd told me she had the tapestry in her trunk.

"Stop fiddle-farting around, Paul!"

"Alright, alright. After I left Marie, I had a chat with my new friend Cliff, one of the buskers in the square. From what I've been able to piece together, Remy was working really late on the night before Guy's murder, and he was dressed as a bronze statue. I think that Remy witnessed the tapestry exchange, and saw both of the parties involved. They must have thought they were alone in the square and that Remy was just another statue."

"Oh, the poor boy," Dottie said. "I guess Remy was just in the wrong place at the wrong time." She kept shaking her head even as she forked chocolate cake into it.

"Remy wasn't exactly an innocent victim," I countered. "He fouled up the tapestry exchange when he took it home for himself. Ultimately, that was what led to Guy's murder. Then the killer must have found out that Remy was a witness, and killed him too."

"So now we know why the murders took place, but we still don't know *who* committed them."

I slurped my coffee thoughtfully. "It had to be Gaillard or Marie, or both of them. Nobody else would've had free access to the dig site at night, especially with round the clock security. Also, Remy would easily recognize them both since Marie runs the museum and Gaillard is probably there every day, too."

"So who do you think it was, Paul?"

"My best guess would be Gaillard Duval. Marie has too much to lose and she's already wealthy. And if she were the tapestry thief, she wouldn't have been so open with me about it's true value, or offered to take me on a tour of the dig site. She didn't have to do any of that."

"You're probably right. So now what?"

I let the question hang in the air as we munched on our cake. I needed to set a trap for the killer, and put an end to this before anyone else got hurt. I could take everything I knew to the police, but we'd already come so far, and I wanted to see it through to the end. Furthermore, I didn't relish the thought of explaining why I hadn't come forward earlier.

Dottie finished her snack and looked at her watch. "We'll have to put a pin in this, I'm running late. I have a can-shaker for my favorite charity." She grabbed her gloves and purse and gave me a quick wave over her shoulder as she rushed out the door.

I stacked our dishes in the sink and heated up a microwave dinner. Cake is great, but I craved something savory. Just two minutes later, I was sitting down to eat. I was barely digging into the part that was supposed to be a brownie, when my phone began to to vibrate across the tabletop.

It was an incoming text from a number I didn't recognize. I stared at the message in disbelief:

Give me the tapestry or someone you know will die.

I felt my stomach drop, but it was from excitement rather than dread. Having a direct line to the killer was a huge break in the case. To start with, I needed to find out where the call came from. And I knew just the person to trace it for me.

Bernard answered on the first ring. "Yell-lo."

There should be a special place in hell reserved for people who answer the phone like that, I thought.

"Hi, Bernard. It's Paul."

"Hey, Paul. What's up?"

"Listen, I just got a weird text from someone and I was hoping you could trace the number."

"No sweat. What's the number?"

I read the number to him, and then listened while he whistled and pecked on a keyboard. He came back to the phone a few minutes later.

"Sorry, Paul. It must have come from one of those throw-away phones. Completely untraceable. What's this all about?"

"I know who the killer is. I'll tell you the whole story later, but for now, I need your help. I'm setting a trap."

"Wow, you can count on me. What do you need?"

"I'll get to that in a second. My plan is to lure the killer into my basement office while I hide near the door. When he takes the bait, I'm going to lock him in and trap him like a rat. I'm hoping he'll have something incriminating on him, like the phone that he sent the text from. It's a gamble, but right now it's all I have."

"It sounds pretty dangerous," Bernard said.

"What can I say? I like to live on the edge. A famous surfer once said that if you want to ride the ultimate wave, you have to be willing to pay the ultimate price."

"And how'd that work out for him?"

"He drowned. But that's hardly the point."

"It most certainly *is* the point, Paul. So where do I come in?"

"I'm setting the trap for 2 p.m., so I'd like you to come over fifteen minutes early and help me spring it."

Bernard sighed into the phone. "Alright, but if

anything goes wrong, we're both going to look like pretty foolish."

As Dottie pointed out, I wasn't the type person who cared about that.

I had a date with a killer.

Chapter 25

I had just less than an hour to set my trap.

I put the rolled up tapestry on the desk in my office and replied to the killer's message: *Tapestry in my basement office 2 pm. I'll be out. Door is unlocked.*

There was no turning back now.

I examined the double doors of my office. I would lock the killer in my office by sliding a broom through the two door handles. By the time he knew what was happening, it would be too late. Then Bernard would call Landry to come and make an arrest. Even if the killer wasn't carrying some incriminating evidence, I was confident that I had enough evidence for the police to build a strong case anyway.

The next thing I had to do was find a good place to hide. It needed to be close enough to the office doors that I could run out and secure them before the killer could react, but not so close that the killer would notice me.

I started to build a wall of boxes next to the office, tall enough to hide behind without having to crouch.

I was so absorbed in my work that I nearly jumped out of my skin when I heard a merry voice behind me. "Hi, Paul!"

I spun around and came face to face with Gaillard dressed in a wide-brimmed hat and a trench coat with the collar turned up. He was smiling, but behind his smile I detected a hint of something evil. Or maybe it was just my imagination? I backed up instinctively. "I didn't expect you until two."

He squinted and tilted his head. "What an odd thing to say. I hope you don't mind that I let myself in. I was a touch anxious."

"No, that's totally fine," I said in a calming voice. "The tapestry is in my office. Help yourself."

"We have lots of time for that." He put his hands on his hips and gazed around the museum, nodding his head. "I adore what you've done to the place! How about giving me the five cent tour?"

Man, this dude is one cool customer! Why is he toying with me?

The last thing I wanted to do was aggravate him, so I indulged his request and rushed him through the exhibits.

I could tell Gaillard was impressed by the work Dottie and I had done, but as our tour progressed, he asked fewer questions and sent more scrutinizing looks my way.

"Are you feeling alright, Paul? You're white as a sheet."

"What? No, I'm fine. Just fine," I said, trying to sound nonchalant. Feeling the need to prove how fine I was, I tried to laugh lightly. But it came off sounding forced and a little maniacal.

Gaillard looked bewildered. "What the devil's wrong with you? Did you hit your head on a surfboard?"

"Ha, good one," I chuckled, nervously licking my lips.

Get a grip, Paul! He thinks you're a lunatic now.

He studied me for a moment, then he smoothed out his moustache and adjusted his tie. He forced a smile, and said, "Let's take a gander at that tapestry now, I'm dying to get my hands on it."

I realized it would be difficult to trap him, since I'd already lost the element of surprise. So I led him to my office and dumped the tapestry in his arms. "Take it and go. As far as I'm concerned, I've never seen it, and I don't even care about the murders."

Gaillard opened his mouth to reply, then closed it. Then he opened it again, and this time he spoke slowly. "Why do you want me to take it?"

"Didn't you come for the tapestry?" I asked.

"You invited me over when you were at the library, remember? I thought I was coming to pass a lovely afternoon with a friend." He set the tapestry down and flung his scarf around his neck. "I'm heading out, Paul; this has been a singularly kooky visit. Mind if I go out the back door?"

"Sure, whatever," I mumbled.

A moment later, I heard him open the steel security door, then slam it shut. The sound was so loud that it echoed around the museum. I made a mental note to put a chain across it so customers wouldn't use it.

Then all at once, I realized what was bothering me about the morning of Guy's murder. Bernard had said he saw someone running to the back of the store, so I assumed the killer had slipped out a few seconds ahead of me. But Tremblay Antiques had the same security door that I did, so if the killer had really fled through it, I would have heard something. This meant that Bernard had lied about seeing Guy's assailant.

I pulled out my phone and looked at the text that Bernard had sent to tell me where my new key was hidden. Sure enough, it came from the same number that the killer had used just a few hours ago. He must have gotten clumsy and used the wrong phone.

I heard the tinkling of the bell over my gift shop door. The tinkling should have been a happy sound, promising paying customers or visits from friends. Instead, it sent a chill down my spine.

Just to be certain, I dialed the killer's number, and heard an electronic chirping coming from the top of the stairs.

I froze.

There was no way I'd make it to the back door since it was located near the stairs. And that was precisely where Bernard was at that moment.

The phone rang again, just around the corner from where I stood. This time the ring was cut short, and Bernard walked around the corner holding his phone to his ear. We faced each other without speaking, then Bernard pulled out a very large gun.

I gulped. When I found my voice, it came out as a weak croak. "Éclair."

Bernard looked confused. "Éclair? What the hell are you talking about?"

"You said you'd drop everything if I said *éclair*."

Bernard looked irritated. "Throw your phone on the ground, Paul."

I did as I was told, but I did it very slowly. I needed time to think.

Locking Bernard in my office wasn't going to happen now, and it was a dim-witted plan to begin with. It was time for a new one. My mind was racing. I found myself studying Bernard's brown leather gloves. I was reminded of my dad's hands, holding his cigarette in his office before all this started. Hardly a month had passed, but it seemed like a lifetime ago. I wondered if I'd ever see those hands again.

Since Bernard was blocking my exit, my only hope was to get to my office and lock myself in. There was no phone line, but at least it would keep me alive for a while longer. Unfortunately, my office was at the far end of the hall. I'd be dead before I took two steps.

I needed to put more distance between us.

"You can have the tapestry," I said, staring at the hole in his gun barrel. "I knew it was you for days and I didn't tell anybody. In fact, I was hoping we could work together. I could use the money."

Bernard shook his head, and said, "Your half-baked mind tricks are as lame as your traps. You really are a screw-up." He sneered when he spoke, reminding me of my brother-in-law Todd. It was true what they say about your life flashing before your eyes.

Bernard must have seen something change in my face. "There it is! The famous temper. I know all about your checkered past. The break-ins, the drug possessions, and the anger counseling. I spent years on the force watching dirt bags like you get off scot-free because of your age. Not this time!" The ends of his mouth stretched toward his ears in a huge sadistic grin.

It was a good thing for me that Bernard had taken this approach. Anger had a mysterious way of clearing my head; it gave me an overwhelming desire to survive, and maybe get a little revenge. Any fear that I felt before was now gone.

I looked at Bernard like he was crazy. "You want to kill me for things I've done in the past? You must have been some policeman. Three murders in one week."

"Just one murder," Bernard corrected. "Yours. And it's going to look like self defense. The other murders will all point to you. I'll tell Landry that I was listening outside Marie's office when she told you the tapestry was worth a million bucks. After that, you killed Remy for it. And since I planted some evidence in Remy's room, it will be an easy sell. All of this happened after you rolled into town, a spoiled slacker with a criminal rec..."

I took off down the hall in the middle of his sentence, bracing myself for a bullet in the back.

"Hey!" Bernard yelled, right before a deafening blast filled the room.

A gunshot in real life was much, much louder than on television. The sound slapped both my ears.

I lunged for the utility panel and hit the main circuit breaker, plunging the basement into darkness. The water heater and furnace became silent, and the faint electrical hum from the wiring stopped completely. Standing still, all I could hear was my own labored breathing.

I heard Bernard's clunky shoes on the floor as he came around the corner, but I couldn't see a thing. I quickly pulled off my own shoes and set them on the floor, careful not to make any noise.

The last thing I saw before the lights went out was my Étienne Brule exhibit. I knew the wax Indian warrior carried a fearsome knife with a really sharp edge, and I desperately needed a weapon.

I held my breath and tiptoed through the darkness on the balls of my feet. I dropped to my hands and knees and crawled into the exhibit, crouching next to Étienne. He smelled like beeswax and old wigs. Even in the dim light, I could see the despair on his face, and for the first time I knew exactly how he must have felt.

Bernard's footsteps grew closer, then his voice cut through the darkness. "Nice move cutting the power, Paul. Good thing I came prepared."

A tiny red light bobbed through the air near the source of Bernard's voice. I deduced that he had a laser sight mounted to his gun. But that wasn't the worst of my problems. My eyes were beginning to adjust to the darkness, and I assumed his were too.

I reached up and tried to pry the knife from the Indian warrior's hand but it wouldn't budge. I twisted the handle with every bit of my strength, until the super-glue broke loose with a loud snap.

In an instant, a red beam flashed in my eyes as Bernard trained his gun on me. "Drop the knife!"

I dropped it, unable to breath, unable to move.

I felt something next to me explode an instant before

I heard the gunshot. I was showered in fine debris that smelled like burnt wood.

"Oops, needs calibrating. I'll compensate in my next shot."

I'd be damned if I was going to give him the chance.

I blasted out of the display like a crazed bull, sending parts of the exhibit and wax figures tumbling into the hall. There was no way I could pass by Bernard, and he was blocking the only path to the emergency exit.

I sprinted the last few feet to my office and heard Bernard right behind me. Another gunshot rang out and a glass display case shattered next to me. I felt the sting of broken glass pepper my face.

I managed to reach my office and lock the double door.

I was caught in my own trap. There was no phone, and the windows were barred. Nobody would hear his gunshots in this stone basement. At least I knew Beachley would be safely hiding upstairs—she was afraid of loud noises ever since some punk kids had thrown firecrackers at her on the beach.

The handle to the door rattled as Bernard tried the lock. Fortunately, the doors swung outward so he wouldn't be able to use his considerable body weight to break them down.

I struggled to catch my breath and think. In surfing, when you're in the middle of a nasty wipe-out, the most important thing is to remain calm. A rough plan popped into my head. It wasn't much better than my last plan, but it was better than nothing. I needed to keep him talking and stall for time.

I raised my voice so that Bernard could hear me through the doors. "Can you answer a few questions for me?"

"So you can stall for time? This isn't a Hardy Boys

novel, Paul." I heard him slump to the floor outside the door, and he was breathing heavily. "Soon as I get my breath back, I'm gonna finish this."

I asked my questions anyway. He was so arrogant that he'd probably welcome the opportunity to toot his own horn. "Where did you get the tapestry? The chest was empty when they dug it up."

Bernard chuckled. "That's because I found the chest first. I work as the night security guard at the dig site. When I saw the half-excavated chest, I figured there'd be something valuable in it. So I grabbed a pick and helped myself. Afterwards, I put the chest back in the dirt just like I found it."

So it was just as Dottie and I had figured, except that it was Bernard instead of Gaillard.

I said, "So you arranged to sell it to Guy, and you hid it for him by the fountain. When your payment never arrived, you assumed he'd ripped you off. You confronted him in his store, and ended up killing him. Am I right so far?"

"Yup," Bernard said. I could hear him putting a fresh ammunition clip in his gun. Now *that* sounded exactly like it did on television.

I took a deep breath and continued, "*You* went out the back door because the front door of Guy's shop was locked from the inside, and you needed his key to open the deadbolt. But here's where it gets weird. I found you outside banging on the front door, so you must have run around the building. Why didn't you just leave?"

"Oh, that," Bernard replied. "I realized I needed to get back inside, otherwise I'd have to explain how my DNA, hair and clothing fibers got there. So yeah, I ran around and made a big show of breaking in."

"So you made sure you were the first one on the scene, and you had me running around chasing shadows. Nice touch by the way. Your description of the killer fit every one of the suspects, including Marie."

Bernard laughed. "Are you finished, Colombo?"

"Almost. We haven't talked about Remy's involvement in all this. This is the part that stumped me, until I sat next to one of those living statues in the town square. When you hid the tapestry in the bushes next to the fountain, you didn't know you were being watched. Remy was there dressed like a bronze statue. He recognized you because he did his act across from the Settlement Museum where you work as a guard. He took the tapestry after you hid it, and then waited to see who came to pick it up. When Guy arrived and left empty-handed, Remy followed him back to his antique store, and must have figured out what was going on."

Bernard said, "Now that I think about it, Guy was confused when I showed up asking for money. I thought he was just being a weasel."

"So you killed him for nothing," I said.

"I guess I did," Bernard said, "but I'm not going to lose any sleep over it. He screwed me over on more deals than I can count, paying me only cents on the dollar. I brought him the best artifacts he's ever seen from the Settlement Museum and the dig site, but he's the only one who ever got rich." He paused. "Now, are there any more questions? I have to be at work soon."

"Just one more. How did you know Remy had the tapestry?"

I could tell I hit a nerve when I heard Bernard stand up. "The punk tried to blackmail me! At first he said he'd sell it to me for fifty grand. I figured it was better than nothing, so I told him to meet me on the path next to the dig site to make the exchange. But he showed up empty handed, said he was going to keep it, and that I should consider the fifty grand to be hush money instead. I told him to stay put while I got the cash, but I came back with a pick-axe instead. Problem solved."

I heard Bernard take a few steps back from the door, then he said, "You know, I was thinking, these locks are pretty good, but they have one weakness."

A series of explosions followed and the door shook as bullets slammed into it. On the fourth shot I heard a metallic clank as the lock was destroyed. By now, my eyes had fully adjusted thanks to a small window above my desk. I knew that once Bernard got into the office he would see me as clear as day.

Before I could finish my thought, he burst into the office, saw me sitting behind the desk, and opened fire. The muzzle flashes were like a strobe light that made the figure behind the desk dance in it's seat. After what seemed like an eternity to my racing brain, Bernard's gun clicked empty.

Only then did he notice the Montreal Canadiens jersey on his victim. "Rocket Richard?" he whispered.

Bernard turned his head when his peripheral vision caught a flash of movement. A sequined arm swung down in a karate chop that connected with his outstretched arm, sending his gun skittering across the floor. He staggered back, off balance and surprised. Next came a powerful uppercut to the jaw that laid him out flat.

I stepped out from behind the door carrying an arm from the wax figure Dottie'd been working on.

"Two more smash hits for Celine," I said out loud, wishing someone had been there to appreciate my wit.

I snatched up the gun and trained it on Bernard, while he pulled himself into a sitting position and rubbed his head.

The lights came back on, and the basement was filled with the sounds of running and shouting. Detective Landry rushed in with Gaillard and several officers. Behind them, I could see Dottie looking extremely upset with her hand over her mouth.

Landry looked at the smashed up dummy behind my desk. It still bore the wax head and blond wig that I'd attached to it minutes earlier. Overall, it was a fairly good likeness of me. Landry turned his attention to Bernard, and then to me and my gun. "What the Sam Hill is going on here? Drop it!"

I dropped the gun and put my hands in the air, breathing heavily.

Bernard found the strength to stand and point a finger at me. "Arrest him! He tried to kill me! And he killed those men. I've got all the proof you need."

Landry reached for his handcuffs and started toward me. I couldn't blame him. It was a lot to process in a short amount of time, and I was the one holding the smoking gun. I held up my hand to stop Landry's progress, and shouted to someone behind him, "Dottie, play the music in the Étienne Brule exhibit."

A few moments later, Bernard Curtius' recorded confession floated through the open door. The looks of confusion on the faces of everyone in the room—except Bernard's—were replaced by surprise and amusement.

"The tape is a three minute loop," I explained. "I hit record when I hid in the exhibit. You should have his full confession there."

Not to mention my Celine comment, I thought proudly.

Landry chuckled as he watched his men arrest a sputtering Bernard. "Alright, I have to admit that's pretty good. Next time, leave the police work to us, alright?"

I gave him my most sarcastic grin. "What next time? We have the lowest crime rate in North America, remember?"

Epilogue

It was the first day of the New France festival.

Dottie was working behind the cash register while Francine helped customers with the merchandise on loan from her store. It was a perfect sunny day with no rain in the forecast for the first time since I'd arrived.

I felt on top of the world. Besides managing to get the gift shop and museum launched, I had enough reservations to keep myself in the black for the rest of the year.

I spent most of the day working with Beachley in the basement. Although it was a self-guided museum, I enjoyed being on hand to answer questions. And truthfully, I just wanted to see people's reactions to the exhibits that Dottie and I had created. Knowing people's likes and dislikes was the best way to know what improvements were needed. The retail side of the business took care of itself since the point of sale software analyzed everything automatically.

"How's it going up here?" I said as I came up the stairs. "I can take over for you guys if you need a break."

Francine was busy with a customer and couldn't respond, but Dottie smiled at me from behind the sales counter. "Oh, don't make a fuss. We're handling things. I haven't had so much fun in years. This is the busiest it's ever been!"

"We have the local newspaper to thank for that," I said. "It certainly doesn't hurt that just last week we were at the center of so much intrigue."

"No kidding! Oh, by the way, I have some bad news." She lowered her voice. "Marie Antoinette was here a few minutes ago. Her hoop skirt took out half of the snow globe section. I just charged her what we paid for them—she had such a regal bearing that I didn't dare upset her."

"They were free, Dottie. I found them in the basement, remember?"

"I know," she said with a grin.

"You did good. She's been persecuted enough."

Today half of the population appeared to be dressed up. Everyone was getting into the spirit of the festival. I doubted there was a single shopkeeper in town who wasn't wearing a costume.

Francine had let out my own costume to compensate for my eating binge, but today it hung loose on me again. I had slashed my calorie intake and resumed my running regiment over the past week, and had lost every ounce of weight that I had put on.

I was amused when Francine showed up that morning wearing a costume that was the matching female version of my own. We looked like an eighteenth-century couple. She claimed it was just to use up the extra fabric, but I wasn't sure I believed her.

Dottie punched some keys to open a sales report on her screen. "Overall, it's been a great start for the day. If this keeps up, we might turn a profit, even without the room rentals."

"A lot of that is thanks to Pascal. If he hadn't gone to bat for us with the city, we wouldn't be open today."

We were interrupted when a young couple brought their purchases to the counter. I left Dottie to take care of them.

Inspired by the sensational events of the past weeks, I had created a special museum display to depict Bernard and his demise. I used some photos of the exhibit to create a large promotional poster for the front window. As I taped it in place, I saw Marie outside the store looking up at my signage. She wore a cream-colored brocade dress and a tall powdered wig. I went outside to greet her. "Not too sensational, I hope?"

She read the sign out loud, *"Quebec In Wax. Experience the violent and dark history of Quebec. Villains, disasters, historical figures."* Then she noticed the new poster in my window and laughed.

It depicted Celine Dion, microphone in hand, giving a karate chop to a cowering Bernard. "Nice job, Paul," she said, shaking her head in wonder. "You're a born showman. P.T. Barnum himself would be proud."

I smiled. "Everyone expects to see Celine Dion, so I'm just giving them what they want. Sort of. We didn't have a lot of time, but we did manage to create a few interesting exhibits. We have a grisly one of the cholera epidemic, and another of King Henri being assassinated in his coach. I even rigged up some animatronics for that one."

"You've been busy! You even found time to solve two murders, and find a priceless tapestry, too." She smiled, and this time it looked sincere.

"The tapestry inspired an exhibit," I said. "It shows the Daughters of the King arriving from France. For the background sound I used girls' voices and waves crashing on a beach. I sampled the voices from the girls at the Crêperie, and had them read from historic diary entries. And in the process, I discovered something pretty incredible; one of the girls at the crêperie is a direct descendent of one of the daughters of the king."

"It sounds fascinating! I expect a grand tour when I have more time. And thank you for returning the tapestry to the museum. It's an incredible artifact, and the story around its discovery has captivated the media. I'm getting calls from all over the world. We had a line-up for admission this morning!"

"We've been super busy here too," I said, "People keep telling me they read about the wax museum in the newspaper, but I haven't had a chance to pick one up yet."

Marie smiled. "I've been plugging your business to the media every chance I get. It wasn't hard, since there's so much overlap in what we do. It's the least I can do, not only because of the tapestry, but because you caught Guy's killer."

"It was a team effort. I couldn't have done it without Dottie."

"I'll make sure to thank her, too."

I shook my head. "It's hard to believe that Bernard was right under our nose the whole time. That time I bumped into him outside your office, he was probably listening at the door."

"Don't get me started on him," Marie said with a sigh. "Looking back at our records, we found a big increase in the number of artifacts that went missing since he was hired."

"I imagine a lot of them were found at Tremblay Antiques."

"Oh, yes, we've recovered quite a number of items already. But some we'll never get back." She looked at her watch. "Sorry, I have to run. I'll be back soon." She smiled again and rushed off.

Just as I turned to go back inside, Napoleon appeared with a young boy in a peasant costume. The boy looked skinny and nervous, and had wire-frame glasses. Napoleon wasn't in costume. He must have figured that since he was the living embodiment of Quebec, there would be no point.

"This is my son Felix," Napoleon said gruffly. "He

wanted to see the museum."

I smiled and shook the boys hand while we all headed into the store, "Hey, little dude, I'm Paul."

"Nice to meet you, sir," Felix replied politely, then he ran down to the museum without saying another word.

Napoleon watched his son disappear with a weary expression, then reached into his pocket. "What do I owe you for admission?"

I waved the suggestion away. "Nothing. There isn't much to see yet, so it's free for now."

Napoleon surveyed the room. I could tell that he was at least a little impressed. "You have a lot of new stuff here. I'll say one thing for you, you're fast."

This was the most civil he'd been since we'd met. We were making progress! I shrugged and replied, "Most of the toys, souvenirs and clothes are from other stores. I still need to order my own merchandise that fits the wax museum theme."

Napoleon looked disappointed. "I guess that means you're planning to stay in town?"

Before I could reply, Detective Landry came through the door wearing an historic military uniform. He greeted us with a smile. "Hey, guys, what's up?"

Napoleon shook Landry's hand, grumbled something unintelligible, and then moved to the other end of the store. When the opportunity presented itself, he didn't waste any time making his getaway.

"Napoleon's son is visiting the museum," I told Landry.

"Ah," he said, smiling while shifting his gaze between us. He seemed to be impressed that a fight hadn't broken out yet. "He must be grateful to you for turning over those divorce papers you found."

"I didn't really have a choice. I wasn't going to steal evidence just to help Marie."

"I appreciate that," Landry said with a wry smile, "but you know what I mean. Napoleon has been nothing but a pain in your ass since you arrived, and thanks to you, he'll probably inherit everything."

I looked over at Napoleon. He was thumbing through a box of Sophie's photographic prints. Satisfied that he was out of earshot, I said, "The truth is, I did give it a lot of thought. Marie is already rich, and Napoleon isn't. Marie was unfaithful, and Napoleon was loyal to Guy for years. But most important of all, that divorce agreement reflected Guy's last wish. We promised to look out for each other, and that was the only chance I would ever have."

"Well, you're a bigger man than me," Landry said, "I'd be out for revenge if I were in your shoes."

"So what's going to happen to Bernard?"

"As you know, he's been charged with two homicides and a laundry list of other crimes. If he's found guilty, and I'm sure he will be, he'll get life in prison with no chance of parole for at least fifty years. Considering his age, he'll never be a free man again."

I shook my head in wonder. "I still can't believe he was capable of that. He seemed so likeable. I guess you really can't judge a book by its cover."

"He had me fooled too, and I worked with him on the force for years."

"That reminds me," I said. "Why did he leave the force? He's too young for retirement, and I couldn't imagine why anyone would give up a policing career without good reason."

"A lot of cops prefer to work in the private sector these days," Landry said. "You can make a lot more money as a private investigator, or offering security services. But in Bernard's case, there was more to it. He was under suspicion for stealing evidence. Nothing could be proved, so he was being pressured out. I guess he wanted to leave on his own terms. Personally, I always thought he was innocent."

My eyes wandered to the cash counter where Dottie was starting to look overwhelmed. "I should get back to work. I'm glad everything worked out."

Landry headed for the door, then stopped. "We'll see you at Pétanque, eh? I talked it over with Napoleon, and he said you could join our group on a trial basis, so as long as you don't annoy him, I guess that makes you an honorary *pure laine,*" he said with a wink.

"I'll be there!" I said, not believing my ears. Will wonders never cease.

I stood in the window and looked out across the street.

I saw Sophie cleaning a table in front of the crêperie. She was dressed as a peasant girl with a white blouse and ankle-length skirt, bustier and an apron. When she noticed me, she smiled and waved.

Suddenly, I had an idea, and I ran up to my room to retrieve something. I returned just as Felix was coming out of the wax museum.

I handed him my skateboard. "You want this? I don't need it anymore."

His face lit up with joy and he nodded eagerly.

For the first time of my life, I was psyched about my future.

THE END

ABOUT THE AUTHOR

 A graduate of the University of Western Ontario, C. F. Carter owns several internet companies and publishes a monthly mystery magazine. When he's not writing, he enjoys badminton, photography, and TV crime shows. He currently lives with his wife and daughter near Toronto, but feels most at home in Old Quebec, where he hopes one day to retire.

Death of a Dummy is his premiere novel in the Wax Museum Mystery series. His website is www.waxmystery.com.

www.ingramcontent.com/pod-product-compliance
Lightning Source LLC
Chambersburg PA
CBHW030250270626
47156CB00021B/1270